HAUNTED HELEN

Mentally scarred by her parents' violent deaths, Helen Sparrow was sent for treatment at a residential psychiatric clinic. Now discharged, she returns to a shadowy old mansion, the scene of both the murders and her repressed, unhappy childhood. But she senses an evil presence in the house: something that follows her along the gloomy halls and whispers just on the edge of her consciousness. Is she insane? Or does some supernatural echo of that terrible night lurk within those walls?

V. J. BANIS

HAUNTED HELEN

Complete and Unabridged

LINFORD
Leicester

First published in Great Britain

First Linford Edition
published 2019

A catalogue record for this book is available
from the British Library.

ISBN 978–1–4448–4047–6

Published by
F. A. Thorpe (Publishing)
Anstey, Leicestershire

Set by Words & Graphics Ltd.
Anstey, Leicestershire
Printed and bound in Great Britain by
T. J. International Ltd., Padstow, Cornwall

This book is printed on acid-free paper

Part I

Helen

1

'Officer,' she said before she said anything else, 'I am haunted. By ghosts.'

It was little wonder, too, after what had happened to her. I thought at the time that she exaggerated.

She did not.

★ ★ ★

A man and a woman were playing tennis, energetically but not particularly well. From three separate windows above, three people watched them. The three were not acquainted. Apart from being in the same hospital, they had no connection with one another. It was mere coincidence that brought them together in this manner and when they moved away from their windows, as each of them did in the next few minutes, their paths would never again cross.

One of them had ceased to pay any real

attention to the tennis players and was remembering instead some news he had just received by telephone. Another was thinking of a woman to whom he had once made passionate love and whose hair was the same auburn color as the man's on the tennis court.

The third, a woman, was thinking of blood, staining clothes and flesh, of the smell of it and the feel of it, warm and wet and growing sticky as it faded from crimson to rust.

'Miss Sparrow?'

Helen turned from the window to find a nurse standing in the open door. She cringed inwardly, as she always did, at the ghastly pink of the nurse's uniform. The outside of the building was pink, too, and even the walls of Helen's room. She had felt more than once as if she were trapped in an enormous bale of cotton candy.

'Your sister is here,' the nurse said.

Helen smiled and followed her out of the room, along the corridor. She was elated that this moment had finally come, but apprehensive as well. A part of her wanted to run, to dash through the lobby and into the freedom that waited beyond the gated doors, but she carefully matched her steps to the nurse's quick little pace. She had learned over the years not to show what she felt. Else she would not now be walking carefully, determinedly, toward that freedom.

'The doctor asked to see you,' the nurse said as they approached Doctor Martin's office door. Helen saw that the door was standing open.

'I thought I was free to go,' she said, stopping abruptly. She felt as if she had somehow been tricked.

'Doctor Martin always says goodbye to his patients and wishes them well,' the nurse said in a voice that hinted at disapproval. Helen ignored that. She was all too familiar with disapproval.

The nurse left her at the door to the doctor's office. Doctor Martin did not get up from his desk as Helen, hesitantly, came in, but he looked up at her and smiled, an unctuous smile. Helen had always disliked his smile. She disliked Doctor Martin, truth be told, though she had always been careful to keep that feeling disguised.

'Helen,' Doctor Martin said belatedly, as if he'd had to search his memory to recognize her. 'So, the day has come at last?'

'Yes,' Helen said, and mentally crossed her fingers. 'Yes, I'm leaving, finally.'

For a moment Doctor Martin looked displeased, and Helen half-expected him to say he had changed his mind about that. What he said instead, though, was, 'Of course, we'll miss you. Where will you be going? Has that been decided?'

'Home,' Helen said. 'I'm going home. I decided that's where I would go.'

Doctor Martin studied her for a long moment. In some ways, Helen did seem like a stranger to him, despite the fact that they had met daily for more than three years. She was a good-looking young woman, in a way, with those large waif-like eyes — too pale a green, as if they had been washed out, but appealing. She was small, too, and slim. The doctor could well imagine that a certain type of man would find her more than a little attractive.

The doctor knew all too well, however, that the surface timidity and the willowy build concealed an iron-hard resolve that had frustrated his most determined efforts to reach her. Indeed, his only success, if success you could call it, had been to return his patient to a speaking state; she had been all but catatonic when she had first come here, unable to speak except in the occasional monosyllable.

She refused, however, to speak of anything of any significance, regardless of how much she was prodded. The doctor liked simpler cases, people who were all of a piece. He had never quite known what to put in Helen's file after he had interviewed her, and even now he had the feeling that there was something more that he should say or do.

Under other circumstances, he might have kept Helen a bit longer at Ville de Valle, for further treatment. He was all too aware that he had not even scratched the surface of the protective armor that this patient wore so steadfastly.

There was a family disagreement going on now, however — over money, as those family squabbles so often were — and for the last few months, the bill had been paid late, later each time, until he had begun to worry that it might not be paid at all.

Ville de Valle was not a charitable institution, but rather a private hospital for those who could afford to pay, and pay dearly. As the hospital's chief administrator, it was a large part of his responsibility to see that those who stayed, paid.

In any event, though he knew that he had done very little for Helen Sparrow, he was convinced that keeping her here any longer would make no great difference in that regard. He smiled at Helen again, stamped her case file 'Closed,' and placed it in the basket for his secretary to file. He did not miss the quick flash of relief that came and went in an instant on Helen's face, as much emotion as she had ever demonstrated.

'Well, I simply wanted to wish you well and good luck,' the doctor said. 'And of course, if you ever need to come back . . . '

'I won't,' Helen said.

They exchanged looks. Doctor Martin nodded and turned his attention to the papers on his desk, dismissing his former patient.

Really, he was glad to be done with her.

*   *   *

Her sister Robbie had come to pick her up. In all the time that Helen had been at Ville de Valle, it had been Robbie alone who had come to visit her. None of the other aunts or uncles or cousins or acquaintances had even sent a card: no 'Get better soon,' or, 'We're sorry for what has happened.'

Helen blinked coming into the bright sunlight outside. In the parking lot, she paused to look back at the ugly pink building in which she had lived for the past several years. Ville de Valle's sign proclaimed it a clinic and a rest home. In fact, it was a mental hospital, very expensive and very discreet.

'I will never come back here,' Helen said aloud.

'Of course you won't,' Robbie agreed with a laugh. 'That's all behind you now. Here's the car.'

'I mean it,' Helen said. 'I'd rather die than have to return to this place.'

'Well, you don't have to return here; and you aren't going to die, not for a long time anyway,' Robbie said. She turned, too, to look back at the building. 'I can't say I blame you. All that Pepto-Bismol pink. It's pretty hideous, isn't it? You know, though, if you got in the car, we could be gone that much sooner, and you wouldn't ever have to see it again.'

They were standing by Robbie's vintage Jaguar. The bright red paint was faded, the seats worn and cracked leather, the convertible top non-existent. 'When it rains, I sit lower and drive faster,' Robbie liked to say, 'and the rain just blows over my head.'

Helen laughed and jumped into the car, and a moment later they were racing down the driveway, taking the curves a bit faster than was probably wise. It felt wonderful to be moving like this, free, with no one trying to restrict her or watching her with judging eyes.

Not that she had actually been a prisoner at Ville de Valle, nor an inmate. Her confinement there had been more or less voluntary, but she understood quite well that there was a confinement that did not depend on bars and locks. She had not been free. That was what it had come down to, and she had been ever aware of that fact.

Now, she was not even alarmed by Robbie's hell-for-leather style of driving. They shot down the expressway at a speed well beyond any legal limit, the noise of the engine and the wind in their faces making conversation all but impossible.

Even when they had left the expressway behind for the gentle curves of Hyde Boulevard, Robbie still driving with an absentminded recklessness, they talked little, though the noise was much less.

'You know,' Robbie said finally, when they were almost at their destination, 'you could come up to New York with me, just for a visit. Give yourself time to get used to things. It's bound to be a lot different for you. Being outside, so to speak.'

'Put off going back to the house?' Helen said. 'That's what you really mean, isn't it?'

'I can't imagine that you're terribly eager to be back there,' Robbie said.

The conversation was interrupted as a big gray Buick pulled in front of them from a side street. Robbie smashed her hand down on the horn button and careened around the offender with a squeal of tires. Helen braced herself stiff-armed against the dashboard until they were in their own lane again, the Buick rapidly disappearing behind them.

'I discussed that with the doctors,' Helen said finally. 'Everyone agreed. If I don't go back to the house now, I'll never be able to. It's like when you're in a plane crash. If you don't go back up right away, before the fear has time to take you over, you never will. If I don't go now, I probably won't ever be able to.'

'Would that be such a bad thing?' Robbie asked. 'Now, don't go getting all defensive, you know I always say what I think. But I'm also the one who stood up for you when you said you wanted to go home, without a chaperone. You do realize that some of the relatives did not exactly like that idea, or, well . . . you know.' Her voice trailed off.

'What you're trying to say,' Helen said, 'is that some of them thought I should just stay at the happy farm.'

Robbie laughed. 'Yes, that was suggested,' she said, and quickly grew more serious. 'And you do realize, I hope, that they could make that happen, if they really wanted to. Relatives can have someone put away permanently without all that much trouble.'

'I've already told you, I won't go back there. Ever,' Helen said, her jaw set stubbornly. 'I'd sooner die.'

'And I've already said you won't have to go back. I would never agree to that if you didn't want to go. I just want you to understand how things are. Aunt Willa, for instance. She'd send you back in a moment if she had a good excuse. And she's not the only one.'

'I know.' Helen sighed and managed a wan smile for her sister. 'And I appreciate what you've done. But, don't you see, that's all the more reason for me to go straight back there, to keep up an air of normalcy. Anyway, truly, I want . . . ' She hesitated. 'I want to bury everything that happened.' She almost added, 'If I can,' and stopped herself. What was important now was confidence, or at least a show of confidence.

'It's a drag, isn't it, having to be afraid of your own relatives?' Robbie said. 'If you can't trust family, who can you trust?'

'It's the money. Money is thicker than blood, isn't it? It brings out the worst in people. And Father left a considerable fortune, didn't he?'

She turned to look at her sister. Robbie's too-long hair was tangled from the wind and her face sunburn-creased to make her look older than she was. She was wearing a battered sweatshirt and driving a beat-up sports car like she was in a hurry to get out of hell. Robbie, who had escaped long ago.

The word stuck in Helen's mind. *Escaped?* As if it had been a prison, and not their home.

14

'Did he leave you any money?' Helen asked aloud.

Robbie's laugh was surprisingly free of bitterness. 'Not a penny. I didn't expect it. He told me when I left I would get nothing unless I came back, and I told him that would never happen, and both of us believed what the other said.'

They had left Hyde Boulevard for quiet, tree-lined Morley Drive. Large old houses, many of them screened from view by the trees and high walls, stood back from the street in elegant isolation from one another and from the world at large. *Established money*, they said. *No nouveaux allowed.*

Robbie slowed and turned into a drive. Helen sprang out to open the wrought iron gates that barred the way and jumped back into the car, picking up the conversation where it had been left off, leaving the gates open behind them.

'You know, of course, anything I have is yours,' she said. 'If you want money . . . '

'I don't need it,' Robbie said. 'I've got a job, for this month at least; and a boyfriend I love; and a great little apartment that I would not for a moment trade for this mausoleum.'

She waved her hand in the direction of the house they were approaching. It was an enormous old house, descending from past regality into a certain musty gloominess. Its cupolas and turrets, its gables and shutters, gave it an atmosphere of long ago; peopled it, one could imagine, with shadows of the past. It was the sort of house, you fancied, that could never truly be empty, however long it went unpeopled.

Robbie brought the car to a skidding stop on the gravel in front of the steps that led up to the big front door. 'The only thing I've ever regretted,' she said, 'is that I didn't take you with me when I went.'

'I was too young,' Helen said. 'Besides, it would have killed Father.' She realized belatedly what she had said and flinched. 'You know what I mean.'

'No, but he would have killed us,' Robbie said. 'Our father was a bastard. I'm sorry, I know, respect for the dead and all that crap, but my respect for him died a long time ago — and not a natural death, either. He killed it, just as surely as those men killed him that night, and I can't pretend otherwise, not even if they sent me to that happy farm . . . oh, shit, I didn't mean anything by that, don't take offense, okay?'

'I won't,' Helen said, but in an absentminded voice. She was looking now at the house before them, at the big paneled door at the top of the stairs. She had hardly even heard what Robbie said.

Robbie got out her side of the car and reached for the suitcase jammed behind the seats; the trunk lid was wired permanently shut. She noticed that Helen had not moved, and asked, 'Are you okay?'

'Yes,' Helen said, but she continued to sit where she was, staring up at the door. She said, 'This is the first time I've been here since that night. I never came back. The entire jury and the court reporters and the judge, everyone came here during the trial, but I didn't. The doctors said it would be too much for me. Doctor Martin told me all about it later.'

Her gaze drifted, across the wide lawn, along the drive up which they had just driven. Everything was neat, well-tended, the grass freshly cut, despite the fact that no one had lived here for years. That is to say, no one had *lived* here.

There was a splash of magenta at the north end of the house: the bougainvillea in bloom. A blue jay flashed across their line of vision, scolding loudly as he went. Everything seemed preternaturally still in his wake.

*   *   *

I think, Officer, that I knew then. Or perhaps I didn't know, but I suspected, I sensed something waiting, and I suddenly thought that it was the house waiting for me. Laughing at me, waiting and laughing.

The children at school used to laugh at me. They called me Crazy Helen, because I never did any of the things they did: the after-school things, the games at the athletic field, the flirtations and the quarrels at the lockers.

18

I hurried home to this house, just as I was doing now, and sitting there in Robbie's car, I had this certainty that any minute the front door would open and there he would be, standing, looking at me in that disapproving way, glancing at his watch to see if I was even a minute late.

Watching and disapproving unnecessarily, actually. There had been only that one time, with the Winslow boy, in the grove of trees behind the school; and truth to tell, nothing had actually happened, there had not been time before we were discovered, sufficiently innocent to be confused about what should be done next. But whatever that was, it had never been done.

He had been informed of it nevertheless — informed, probably, of more than was factually true — and ever since, every day, he waited and timed me. As if that might happen again. As if . . .

And then, while I sat in the car staring at the door, it suddenly, horribly, did open. I shrank back into the worn leather. The unexpectedness of it, the awful *things I had been imagining. I wanted to cry out.*

Instead of my father, however, it was a tall, plump woman with silver hair and a pink face who stood in the doorway.

2

'There's Mrs. Hauptman,' Robbie said.

Helen got out of the car and came up the steps with Robbie, so happy to see a familiar face that she could almost pretend she and the housekeeper had been fond of one another in the past.

'Mrs. Hauptman, hello, how good to see you,' she said.

Standing at the door, watching them come up the stairs, Mrs. Hauptman looked anything but happy to see them.

'They told me you had decided to stay here,' she said.

'Yes, and I'm so glad you agreed to come back to look after things. It's good to see someone I know.'

'You have to understand, I can't come full-time,' the housekeeper said, stepping aside for them to come into the hall. 'I can come mornings and all day Wednesday if you want me, but I can't come full-time and I won't come evenings.

Mister Hauptman says he will not fix his own supper, regardless. I wouldn't have come at all, to be honest, but Miss Roberta said she couldn't get anyone else to even set foot in the place, and I thought there ought at least to be someone here to help out. But it's only part-time. No offense meant, of course.'

'And none taken,' Helen said with a smile, but the moment had gone a bit flat. She paused inside the door to look around.

'Well,' she said. They were both watching her and trying not to show it. She knew that it was important that she act as if everything were normal, as if she looked at ease and unconcerned, but her heart was pounding wildly in her chest.

She went to the foot of the stairs, thinking she should climb them, and she actually had put one foot on the lowest step and taken hold of the banister, but she stopped then and looked down at her hand. She was glad her back was to them, to give her time to catch her breath.

She said again, 'Well.'

'I guess he won after all,' Robbie said.

She set Helen's suitcase on the black and white tiles, and looked around as well.

Helen made herself take a deep breath. 'Who won?' she asked, turning.

'Father. I said I'd never again set foot in this house, and he said I would. And, here I am. So, he won, didn't he?' She gave Helen a concerned look. 'Are you okay? You look like hell.'

A flood of emotion rose within Helen, threatening to burst through the dam that she had erected within herself, and for a moment she almost said something; but she knew that it was Robbie who had championed her sanity, her freedom, who had made it possible for her to be released and to come home. If Robbie lost confidence in her, she could find herself going back to that horrible pink building, and that she could never bear.

She glanced at Mrs. Hauptman. For the moment the housekeeper's attention was focused on some speck of dust she had spied on the little gate-legged table against the wall, and she seemed entirely unaware of Helen.

When they had been children, Helen

and Robbie had played the game of 'Freeze.' One of them would say, at any time, 'Freeze,' and they both of them had to freeze in whatever position they were in at the moment, until the caller said, 'Melt.' Presumably if 'melt' was never called, they might have remained frozen in those positions through all eternity.

'We're just playing freeze,' Helen told herself in those horrible seconds while she stood at the foot of the steps, and they might indeed have remained frozen through eternity in the positions in which they were just at the moment: Mrs. Hauptman, bringing the full weight of her Germanic disapproval down on that unsuspecting piece of dirt; Robbie, beginning to fidget, clearly wanting to be on her way and out of the house she had always hated, and at the same time wanting to do her duty by her sister; and Helen herself, trying not to react to the blood on her hands, blood from the banister, wet and red and making her stomach give a threatening turn.

'Look, love,' Robbie said, coming across the hall to stand in front of her sister and take Helen's hand in her own, 'I don't exactly have to get back into the city tonight. I mean, I could call Joe and tell him I'm staying over, he'll be cool with that.'

Helen gave her head a toss. 'Oh, don't start making a big fuss over me,' she said. 'I'm all right, really, I swear I am. I'm not afraid, and Mrs. Hauptman is here if there's any problem.'

'I can't stay nights,' Mrs. Hauptman said with emphasis. 'Mister Hauptman likes his supper on the table when he gets home. I'll be here by nine in the morning, and I'll leave at noon, except Wednesday. I can stay till four on Wednesday. But I came this afternoon because you were coming home. I thought I ought to be here.'

Helen hardly heard her, and didn't think it mattered much anyway. Clearly, Mrs. Hauptman had not seen the blood, nor had Robbie. And now that she looked down at her hands, neither did she. It was gone. She had only imagined it, in the stress of the moment, and she could never, ever tell them, or anyone, that she had seen it, or how frightened she had been.

'Tell you what,' she said aloud, managing a cheerful grin, 'how about if I take this bag upstairs and get rid of it, and we'll have some coffee before you go, okay?'

'Sounds good to me,' Robbie said, obviously relieved that her overnight presence wouldn't be needed after all.

'I'll make coffee,' Mrs. Hauptman said, and left them for the kitchen.

Robbie looked around again, and seemed about to suggest that she come up with Helen, but she changed her mind. She was, after all, the champion of independence. And she knew, as well as Helen did, how important it was that everything be as normal as possible.

'I'll be in the den,' she said instead, and went toward it, walking briskly, the way she always had.

Helen watched her go, then turned back to the stairs and started up them. She did not take hold of the banister again, however, but leaned as far away from it as she could, actually brushing her shoulder along the wall.

She could not keep her eyes from the carved wooden railing, nor from the crimson stains glistening everywhere on its polished surface.

Blood. Everywhere, blood, up and down the carpeted stairs, dripping from the banister, staining the silk-covered walls with scarlet handprints.

3

I think there is a lure to evil. Don't you agree, Officer? We may be attracted to goodness or virtue on an intellectual level. We may even want those attributes, in ourselves or, certainly, in others.

Wickedness has its own appeal though. The books we read, the shows we watch at the theaters or on television, are more often than not the violent ones, aren't they? Of course, we like to say it's the drama that is important, but, really, that's just kidding ourselves, isn't it? It is the violence that fascinates us, the murder and bloodshed, the horror. Deep within ourselves, some silent stream flows in rhythm with those evil currents. Despite our best natures, we are drawn to the evil man, the evil woman. Surely Shakespeare took more pleasure from his lustily wicked Iago than from dreamy Desdemona.

I think that I knew all along, from the

*first moment I arrived home, that some-
thing evil dwelt in that house, was in
possession there. And that knowledge both
frightened and fascinated me.*

★　★　★

'Do you think you should have a drink?
You've got a long drive ahead of you.'

Robbie had gone to the bar to get
herself a Scotch. She shrugged and
poured generously into her glass.

'That Jag could find its own way home
by this time,' she said. 'All I've got to do
is sit and hold on.'

Helen was seated stiffly in one of the
chairs, sitting on the edge of it, sipping
her coffee. Mrs. Hauptman had returned
to her kitchen. Faintly in the distance
they could hear the clatter of dishes and
pans.

'Maybe you should have a drink
yourself,' Robbie said. She reached for
another glass. 'It would do you good. You
look all keyed up.'

Helen gave a shake of her head. 'I
couldn't,' she said.

29

'Why not? You know, there's no one now to tell you what you can and cannot do.'

'Yes, that's true,' Helen said. 'You know what's funny? I actually miss that. You get used to things, you know. I suppose, really, habits are stronger than love, if you think about it. All those years, him coming into the room to tell me what to do, what to wear, what to think. Sometimes I feel — oh, I don't know. I suppose *unattached* is the word I'm looking for.'

Robbie brought her a glass of whiskey. Helen took it obediently, but made no move to drink from it.

'You still have me,' Robbie said.

'That's not much, is it?' Helen said and looked immediately embarrassed. 'Oh, I don't mean that the way it sounded. I love you dearly, you know that. I just mean, that's all that I do have. There's nothing, no one, apart from you. And this house, of course, and all that money, but nothing else. Other people have husbands and wives and boyfriends and enemies, even. Old friends. Schooldays memories.

Class rings, even. I have nothing.'

'I wouldn't be so cavalier about 'all that money,' love; there's some as would be glad to take it off your hands. As for the rest of it, you have to get out and make friends, is all,' Robbie said.

The conversation was too grim for her. She avoided thinking of serious things as much as she could. She'd been serious enough in the past, in this house, to last her a lifetime. 'It's not as hard as it seems. Here's to living free,' she said, and lifted her glass in a toast.

Helen raised hers too, and took a tiny sip from it. She wasn't used to liquor, had never cared for it much, and it burned her mouth when she swallowed. She said, more as if she were thinking aloud than speaking to her sister, 'I used to think that it was because of him that I wasn't. Free, I mean.'

'Well it was him, of course,' Robbie said. 'I'd never have been free either if I hadn't left. And he wouldn't let you be, especially not after I'd gone.'

'No,' Helen said with a shake of her head. 'If it had been him, I'd have been set free, wouldn't I, when he died?'

'But you've been at that, that place,' Robbie said. 'You've been confined for three years.'

'I'm not sure that matters much, really. Confinement, freedom — they exist, they have their essence, within the individual, don't they, independent of any outside master? There were patients at Ville de Valle who were quite free, in their own ways. And there are people out here who never are. At least, that's how it seems to me. I don't think those pink walls made any difference.'

Robbie had been looking at her over the rim of her glass. She took a long drink now, not much liking the drift of this conversation. She was fond of her sister and she felt sorry for her, for what had happened to her, but she could never quite free herself of a sense of guilt, either.

She had never rid herself of a conviction that when she ran away, when she escaped this house and their tyrannical father, she had made things worse for Helen. All of that man's formidable temper, his cruelty and his bullying, had been directed then at Helen, who had been only thirteen at the time. Robbie's freedom had always been poisoned by the notion that it was purchased at the cost of her sister's enslavement.

Except with her shrink, though, she had never discussed this belief with anyone, and it made her uncomfortable now to talk about what Helen had experienced in that interim. She finished off the rest of her drink and set the glass down on the bar with a loud bang.

'Well, if I'm going, I'd better hit the road,' she said. 'You sure you don't want to change your mind and come with me? Joe won't mind, and the sofa-bed's actually pretty comfortable.'

'I'm sure,' Helen said, standing too. She put her own drink aside, barely touched, and walked Robbie out to her car. She had an urge to hold on to her sister, to delay her departure, but she resisted that.

'Really, it will be kind of nice to be by myself for a change,' she said aloud, partly to convince Robbie and partly to convince herself. 'All that time, people watching you constantly. You can't imagine.'

'I guess it will be a relief for you. I hadn't thought about it that way. It must have been horrible.'

'It was.'

They shook hands at the car. Helen would rather have embraced, but she was not the one to initiate such an intimate gesture, and Robbie made no move to do so. She got quickly into the car instead, fired it up, and in a moment she was roaring down the driveway, waving once before she disappeared onto the street. She left the gates standing open, as she had always done. Helen strolled down the drive to shut them with a noisy clang. As she used to do also.

She paused on the way back up the drive and looked at the house. Had she made a mistake by staying here? Perhaps she should have gone into the city with Robbie.

She wrinkled her nose at that thought, however. Something prudish within her had recoiled at that suggestion when Robbie had first made it. Sleeping on a sofa while in the very next room, Robbie and a man Helen had never even met, were . . . she couldn't even think what exactly it was they might be doing, but even the vague thought of it made her uncomfortable.

She supposed she was jealous, though not in the way one might suppose. Not jealous because Robbie had found someone to love, someone who loved her. If anything, she was glad for her. It was Robbie she was jealous of, but she could not understand that either.

She had always adored her older sister. And many nights they had shared the same bed, Robbie getting up from hers to clamber into Helen's, or Helen the one to make the trip. The tight embraces in which they clasped one another, however, had not been sexual in nature. They had clung to the only thing solid and safe in their lives, had found in one another the only comfort, the only solace they knew as children.

And Helen could not imagine sleeping on a sofa, alone, hearing the sounds that she felt certain she would hear from the bedroom in which Robbie and her friend shared a bed, in a way like she and Robbie had once shared theirs, and at the same time differently, too.

She knew that it was strange that she had reached adulthood with so many attitudes that even she knew were prudish and old-fashioned. Of course, that was her repression at her father's hands.

There were times, though, when she thought that her father had perhaps been justified. There had been occasions, so very many of them, when she had found herself thinking of wicked things, things she knew were wrong for a girl to think about.

Though she had never had more than a vague idea of what was being suggested, that Winslow boy had hardly had to coax her into the woods that day after school, and she had many, many times thought with regret of the interruption that had prevented her discovering what was intended.

It had often seemed to affirm her father's accusations that she was a wicked girl. In her own fantasies, she could see that she was. She had tried to fight against those, to overcome that part of her nature, to bend herself to her father's will, to embrace what she could see was 'goodness.' Or, at least, what her father defined for her as goodness.

Of course, as she had gotten older, she had acquired a certain intellectual freedom. There had been an extensive library at Ville de Valle, and there had been many books on sexuality. It was a subject to which she had given almost no thought until Doctor Martin had begun to ask those embarrassing questions. At first, she had found them literally incomprehensible. She had no idea what it was to which the Doctor was alluding.

When she had finally realized their point, she had been first shamed and later angry, but in time, curiosity had come to the fore, and she had begun to sneak books out of the library, and to read them late at night in the sanctuary of her room.

She had come to see that the sexual impulse was not 'a disease,' as her father had once called it, nor even necessarily a wicked thing.

She had been early and well indoctrinated, however, into other attitudes, and one part of her continued to be embarrassed by the feelings that she now saw she had always carried within her.

She could only conclude that her father was entirely right. She had been a wicked child.

* * *

Mrs. Hauptman had prepared an early dinner for her and laid it out in the dining room: cold roast beef and a green salad and apple pie. It was fast coming on to evening and the housekeeper was preparing to take her leave. She seemed, though, to experience a certain remorse at going.

'So, you really are going to stay here by yourself, then?' she asked. She was at the kitchen door, her purse over her arm, but she paused with her hand on the knob.

'Yes, of course,' Helen said. When Mrs. Hauptman still hesitated, she added, 'It's quite all right, really. I'm not frightened of staying here alone.' It was not altogether true, but complete honesty was a luxury she had never been able to afford.

'I guess lightning isn't going to strike twice,' the housekeeper said, a not altogether comforting assessment. She pulled the door open. 'Well, then, goodnight. I'll be back in the morning. At nine.' And she was gone.

'Goodnight,' Helen said, but she found herself addressing the closed door.

She went back to the dining room and sat down to eat the dinner that Mrs. Hauptman had prepared. The food at the clinic had been no more than adequate, and she knew from past experience that Mrs. Hauptman was an excellent cook, so she supposed that this was delicious, but although she ate slowly, she tasted nothing.

She was only putting off what she knew that she would have to do eventually, and she scarcely paid any attention to her meal. From time to time she paused with her fork in the air, halfway from plate to mouth, and cocked her head, listening.

She heard nothing. The silence was complete, excessively so, the sort of silence that gives the impression of someone holding his breath. The house seemed to be doing just that, holding itself in abeyance. No curtain rustled, no old floorboard creaked as, in a house of this vintage, it ought to have done.

She gave up finally and, with a sigh, pushed her plate aside. She must lay the ghosts at once if she was ever to relieve the tension that had been building steadily within her since she had arrived home.

She went into the hall, to the stairs. The banister was clean, brightly polished, not a trace of blood on it. And, really, how could she have ever imagined otherwise? As if Mrs. Hauptman would have permitted that, would have allowed any souvenirs of that night to remain.

She climbed the stairs slowly, ceaselessly scanning the steps and the carpet and the walls. They were impeccably clean, every stain gone. There was nothing to tell the tale of the grisly events that had happened here, in this house, on these stairs.

She had seen her own room earlier, when she brought her suitcase up, and she knew that it was fine. Nothing had actually happened there, though it had threatened. It was her parents' bedrooms that drew her now, their separate rooms. Her father had not shared his wife's bedroom for many years.

'We must set an example for the children,' he told his wife when she questioned that arrangement.

Moreover, he was a man of boundless energy, rarely stilled, and often he worked through the night, sitting at his desk, poring over his accounts, and his wife would hardly have had a night's rest while he did so, as he had pointed out to her.

So, she had been moved to the small bedroom at the end of the hall, that had originally been a maid's room, and the largest of the upstairs rooms had been made into his combination bedroom and office. It was the first room at the head of the stairs. Helen went there first.

There was a faint, scurrying sound as she opened the door. Mice, she supposed. It was hardly surprising that they had made free with the house in the time that it had sat empty. But when she looked in, there was nothing to be seen, and once again, the house had fallen eerily silent.

The last time she had seen this room, it

had been a shambles: tables upended, lamps broken, even the draperies at the windows pulled down and lying in a heap at the foot of the window. And, snaking across the floor, a crimson trail that led to the hall and down the stairs.

Of course everything was clean now, the stains gone, the furniture righted.

Although he had been over fifty at that time, her father had been big and strong. He had been taken by surprise at his desk by four young men, young men in their prime who were armed with guns and knives, and you might have thought that he would have succumbed to their attack in a moment, but they had barely been his match.

He had broken from the room and nearly made it to the front door, from all indications dragging his assailants with him, before they finally felled him. He had lost most of one hand in the initial attack, and that had been left behind in the office, on the floor by his desk. He had fought his way to the hall with pieces of finger and flesh and tendon dangling from the stump of his wrist.

They had struck him repeatedly in the back of the head with something — a hammer, the police surmised — and they had shot him at least seven times, and still, he had almost reached the front door, as if something more than human, some supernatural force, had driven him.

In the violence of his struggles, he had saved Helen's life, although Helen had not supposed for an instant that this had been his intention. It was the shouting and cursing, the crashing of furniture and the gunshots that carried across the wide lawns to old Mrs. Danver's driveway, where she was walking her Pekinese.

Alarmed, she had called the police, and they had arrived in time to save Helen from what would otherwise have surely been a similar fate. So, her father, who had never really shown her any affection, had saved her life. She owed the man that, at least.

The police had not arrived in time, however, to save Helen's mother. She died sometime between her husband's death and the pounding of the police at the front door.

Helen left her father's office and went down the hall, to the last room, the one that had been her mother's. It was at the back and though it was small, it had the advantage of a large window that over-looked the lawn with its goldfish pond and the mournful willow that hung over it.

She hesitated at the door to the room, however. She had not been inside this room that night nor since, and she did not in fact know what had happened beyond this door, but she knew that it had been horrible indeed.

She reached for the knob, and at the last moment, brought her hand back. She could not after all go inside. Some primitive fear held her back, notwith-standing that common sense told her every trace of what had happened in the room had surely been erased from there just as it had been elsewhere throughout the house. For all that she assured herself of that, however, she could not quite bring herself to take hold of the knob and open the door.

She stood and stared at it, and again it

seemed to her as if she heard sounds from within: vague, indefinable sounds, like the rustle of dried leaves in the wind. Or secretive, whispering voices. She found herself wondering what those voices could possibly be saying, and to whom.

Gradually she became aware of a chill that crept over her. It was a warm enough evening, and she had felt nothing like this elsewhere, but before this door, it was cold, almost freezing. An icy wind seemed to blow just along here, but when she turned her head this way and that, there was no draft; the air was not moving. That awful chill might have risen from the floor itself. Or from the room beyond the door.

Someone suddenly knocked loudly, making her start.

'Who on earth?' she said aloud. It was evening, and since she had come upstairs the house had settled into near darkness, as if it were sinking into an abyss.

She started for the stairs, but stopped at the door to her own bedroom. The knocking was coming from within there, and not from the front door.

There was no one here, in the house

with her. Robbie was long gone, and Mrs. Hauptman had left for the day. She was alone in the house, and yet there was the knocking again. Tap, tap, tap, and a pause, and tap, tap, tap, coming from within her bedroom.

She opened the door. The bedroom was dark within. The lamps were across the room, one on the dresser on the far wall, and one on the nightstand between the twin beds.

She tried to bring herself to step into the room, to ask, 'Who's there?' but fear held her in check. Something moved in the faint light coming through the window, blocking the light for a moment. She had a nearly uncontrollable urge to urinate.

Then, in a flash, she understood, and let out the breath she had been holding, her shoulders slumping. She stepped into the room, crossed to the dresser, and turned on the lamp there, and went to the window, where an errant shutter was blowing in the wind.

She opened the window, leaning out to take hold of the shutter and fasten it back. The knocking ended.

She left the light on and went back to the hall, and downstairs to finish her supper. She felt the whole time as if someone were watching her.

4

I had the impression that there was something there in the house with me, some evil presence that followed me along that shadowed hall and whispered just out of the range of my hearing, something vague that I could not put my finger on.

I did not try, though, to name it, nor think why it was there. I did not want to know. But I was aware of it, always there, always following me.

At first, there was nothing concrete that I could describe, nothing happened. Until that business with the beds . . .

* * *

She had been there for several days, without incident, when Helen woke one night from a bad dream that fled her memory at once and only left her a lingering sense of unease. She lay for a moment, staring up at the ceiling, invisible in the darkness, and it came to her gradually, a feeling that she was not alone in the room.

Unmoving, she strained her ears at the silence. At first, she heard nothing, but then she became aware of faint noises that she could not identify, coming from the other bed in the room.

That had been Robbie's bed and it had never been removed when Robbie had left home. Year in, year out, it had remained exactly where and how it was, always neatly made up for the sleeper who no longer occupied it.

Now, though, Helen grew increasingly certain that someone did occupy it. It sounded as if someone were in that bed, someone who slept badly, tossing and turning, the breathing increasingly heavy.

It gave her a feeling of horror, to think that someone was in the very room with her. Not just in the house, where she had believed she was completely alone, but here, in this room, in the bed no more than five feet away from hers. The bed into which she had so often crept, to cling to the safety of her sister's embrace. But whatever was there, it was surely not safety it offered.

She felt physically ill, and so terror stricken that for long moments she was unable to move at all. She lay as if some great weight was upon her, pressing her down, crushing the air from her lungs until she could scarcely draw a breath. Her thoughts chased here and there, settling nowhere, like leaves before an autumn wind.

It was no use, though. She knew she would have to move, would have to see for herself what was in the room with her. It took all the strength, all the courage that she could summon just to turn her head, to look in that direction. She had left the curtains pulled back, and the waxing moon cast its faint light through the window.

Her bed creaked faintly as she moved.

She looked toward the other bed, the bed that should have been empty, and as she looked, something happened, so sudden and so startling that her heart actually seemed to stop beating.

Someone sat up in her bed. Not in Robbie's bed, nearby, but in her own bed, directly beside her.

She gave a little bleat of terror and, rolling and kicking at the bedclothes that seemed like so many fingers clutching her legs, she half-leaped, half-fell out of the bed on the opposite side.

The lamp on the nightstand was between the two beds and she could not have reached that without reaching across whoever was in her bed, but there was another lamp on the dresser and she flew to it, almost knocking it over in her frantic search for the pull chain. Her entire body jerked spasmodically with the fear that zigzagged through her as the light came on. Her eyes wide in terrified anticipation of what she would see, she looked back at the bed.

There was nothing there.

Nothing.

She stood, clinging with one hand to the edge of the dresser, and looked slowly around the room, but there was no one else in it. She went to the other lamp, on the nightstand, casting apprehensive glances over her shoulder as she went, and turned that one on too, and looked again around the bedroom.

The room was empty. So far as the naked eye could see, in any case. There were places where someone could hide, of course, and she told herself that she ought to look more carefully. In the closets, for instance, or under the beds. But she knew that she could never summon the courage to kneel down, to lift the bedclothes, and look into the darkness beneath.

She hadn't the courage either, though, to turn out the lights and go back to bed. It was obvious that she had been dreaming, that when she thought she was awake, she was not, not fully, and her dream had lingered into the waking state, and the line had blurred between sleep and wakefulness.

She had been under a strain, and nervous about being back in the house, and being alone for the past few days; and hadn't her father criticized her often in the past for her tendency to fantasize?

No doubt these were explanations enough, but none of them made it possible for her to go back to bed, and there was no possibility of her going back to sleep. She was too frightened of perhaps repeating the experience. It seemed as if she could almost sense the dream lingering in one of the shadowy corners of the room, waiting to take possession of her again should she fall back into sleep.

She could not even bear the thought of turning off the lights, but left them glaring brightly. The room had turned cold, though it had been a warm night when she went to bed. She got a blanket from the bed.

Standing by the bed, in the few seconds it took to tug the blanket free from the twisted sheets, she had the horrible feeling that a hand would reach out any minute from under the bed and grab hold of her bare ankle.

It was absurd, she told herself. She was being a fool, but she nevertheless stood as far away from the bed as she could manage and leaned at an awkward angle to get the blanket.

There was a small chair, slip covered in

an endless pattern of faded violets, sitting against the wall by the dresser, in the full light of the lamp there. She went to sit stiffly on it and wrapped the blanket about herself.

The clock on the nightstand told her it was nearly four o'clock in the morning. It could not be light before seven, surely. She did not relish the thought of sitting for all that time in the uncomfortable little chair, waiting, but she could still not quite rid herself of the feeling that there was someone else in the room with her.

Lightning flashed at the window and there was a distant crash of thunder. A storm had come up. That no doubt explained the coldness in the room. She was aware now of the wind that blew outside. It howled and whistled and huffed like a host of phantom riders rushing through the trees, and the house answered their calls with groans and creaks. It was impossible not to think one heard footsteps in the hallway outside the door. She found herself staring hard at the door, expecting it to open suddenly.

She closed her eyes, trying to close her

mind to these thoughts, but she could not help hearing the beating of her heart, and she fancied that it might stop at any minute. Her breathing sounded ragged and labored, and she was convinced that there was something wrong with her lungs.

The reasoning part of her mind told her she was being silly. She had regularly undergone at least basic medical examinations at Ville de Valle. Her mysterious ailments would disappear with the dawn. For the moment, though, they refused to be put aside.

In time, her breathing began to return to normal and her pulse slowed. The frozen tension drained from her shoulders and they slumped a little. She still could not think of going back to sleep, but at least she was no longer overwhelmed by fear. She could even laugh at herself a little for the violence of her reaction to what had been, after all, only a very bad dream. And she had her cellphone — there it was, on the nightstand. But who could she call? And what could she tell them? 'I had a bad dream . . . '

It was not hard, either, to imagine how she had come to dream it. This was how that night had begun for her, wasn't it, that awful night? It had begun with the realization that someone was in her room.

That time, it had been no dream, but real, and nothing so vague as an indistinct figure sitting up in bed beside her. It had begun with a hand on her shoulder, shaking her awake. She remembered reaching, still half-asleep, for the lamp on the nightstand, and saying aloud, as she started to sit up, 'Father?'

Someone seized her hand in a rough grip, though, before she could turn on the light, and a deep baritone that was certainly not her father's said, 'Don't move.'

She was shocked into wakefulness. Half-sitting, she cowered back against the headboard. It was a full, blatant moon and there was light enough to see clearly. What she saw was a man, a stranger, in a Hawaiian print shirt and with a full, shaggy beard, leaning over the bed.

She saw too the knife the man held in his hand, its blade gleaming wickedly in the moonlight. It was a huge knife, it looked like the swords the knights carried in one of her childhood picture books. Later, she would learn that it was a machete, but for now she was only aware of how dangerous it looked.

The stranger gestured with it toward the empty bed. 'Where's he?' he asked.

Helen was surprised that her voice, when she answered, sounded so normal. 'She. That's Roberta's bed. She hasn't lived here for years.'

The man looked at her as if judging her truthfulness. After a moment, he turned on the light himself and looked around the room. He went to the closet and opened the door. It struck Helen as funny: did he think Robbie was hiding in there? Despite the seriousness of the situation, it made her giggle.

Startled, the stranger whirled about. Helen was silent then, staring at him with wide eyes. Even without that enormous knife, he would have been scary. He had a frightening quality, a wildness about him, like a savage beast. Helen shrank back under the covers as the man came back to the bed and leaned over her. He brought the knife down so that its point just touched the skin at Helen's throat.

5

'Don't make a sound,' the man with the knife said. His eyes, catching the light from the lamp, gleamed in an eerie, a demonic way. 'Wait here. Not a sound. I'll be back. And don't try to leave, either. Don't move.'

He stole noiselessly into the hall, closing the door quietly after himself. For several minutes Helen did not move at all, taking him literally, but remained exactly where she was, cringing against the headboard.

After a time, though, her arms grew stiff from the unnatural position and she let herself sit up. Finally, she slipped out of the bed. She tiptoed to the door and listened, but she could hear nothing beyond it.

She had no idea what was going on out there, but she could not bring herself to open the door either to find out. Instead, she went to the window seat. With the full moon it was nearly as light as day outside. She found herself remembering all those old horror stories that had so frightened her as a child. Vampires and werewolves and demons, cavorting by the light of the full moon.

And they had come true, hadn't they, those grisly tales? Surely the man who had come into her room was a demon of some sort. Helen sat at the window seat and waited to see what horrors would ensue.

Afterward, although little of it reached her at Ville de Valle, there was much controversy in the newspapers as to why she did not simply leave her room, go down the stairs and escape the house. As it turned out, she would have had ample opportunity to do so while the intruders were occupied elsewhere with her parents.

She would not even have had to summon that much courage. There was a trellis just outside the open window, and certainly she knew that it provided a means of exit from the bedroom. Robbie had used the same means many times over the years before she left the house for good. With Helen holding the curtains aside for her, Robbie would crawl out the window, clamber down the trellis into the night, going to assignations the exact nature of which Helen had been unable to quite comprehend then, though in time she came to realize that Robbie was meeting men, doing things that only much later Helen would imagine excitedly.

The question of why Helen did nothing, however, was never satisfactorily answered, not in the newspapers nor in the courtroom, where it was asked as well. Of course, no one ever asked it directly of her, not even the doctors at Ville de Valle, though they did tiptoe gingerly around the subject on more than one occasion.

There were theories and counter-theories. Most of them concluded that she had been rooted to the spot by a fear that affected her reasoning faculties; but none of the theories ever seemed quite satisfactory to explain it.

Even had she been asked, Helen could

probably not have explained it any better. That she had her reasons for inaction was certainly true, but they were so intimate, and she was so used to repressing certain kinds of feelings, that she was at the time only dimly aware of her thoughts; and afterward she carefully gathered them up and locked them away in one of those dark rooms of her mind that she kept closed off to all intruders.

She was twenty-five years old, and although she was a good-looking young woman, she was in every sense a virgin. She had never experienced any sexual activity except her infrequent solitary explorations, which so consumed her afterward with guilt and shame.

In nearly every sense — physically, chronologically, legally — she was a grown woman, but she had hardly experienced life at all. She had never had any kind of adventure, had never gone out for an afternoon or evening without her father's permission, nearly always in her father's company. She had never prepared a meal for herself; had not, in fact, ever eaten one alone before she had returned just recently to this house, nor ordered anything for herself from a menu — that too had always been done for her, by her father. She had never picked out a dress or a pair of shoes for herself, had never traveled anywhere except two or three times into the city, in her father's watchful company.

In her entire life, she had never had an opportunity to make a wrong decision; everything that had ever happened to her had been carefully planned and rigidly dictated by her father — until that night.

She sat in the cold moonlight at the window seat, listening to the clamor that erupted outside her room, heard the shouting and the shots and the crash of furniture being tossed about, and she did nothing.

If she had been asked, she would certainly have admitted that she hated her father, but that was not why she remained immobile. It was not fear that kept her frozen in place, though she was certainly frightened. Nor did she wish her father to lose the fight that was so obviously now being waged for his life, not any more than she wished to lose her own life, which she did not.

The simple truth was, the thought of escaping or even of trying to help her father in his struggles never so much as crossed her mind. As she had been all her life, she was only a witness to events, a listener, afraid and waiting for someone else to tell her what to do.

But these thoughts, ill-formed and so insubstantial that she herself was hardly aware of them, she could never have shared with anyone.

There was worse, though. It is true that while the intruders were violently attacking and murdering her father, she had not only done nothing, but she had *felt* virtually nothing. Except for her fear for her own safety, she heard it all play out without emotion.

That much, at least, she could face afterward; but when her mother died, she did feel emotion. She did not know, then nor now, exactly how her mother died. Probably, she never would know, but she knew that it had been horrible beyond description.

And, here was the worst, the most shameful of all: while it was happening, while she knew that it was horrible, she had been moved not by pity, not by grief, but by resentment. Resentment not of her killers, but of her mother, because her death had interfered. Though in what it had interfered, she was never clear even in her own mind.

In something, surely. Something had been intended to happen, to her. Now she would never know what it was that those men had intended for her. The first true adventure of her life, and it had been thwarted before it happened.

When the bearded man in the Hawaiian shirt came back, there was another man with him, thin and stoop-shouldered, who never stopped smiling, as if he found this strange adventure totally amusing.

Helen got to her feet when they came in. It seemed like hours since the noise of the struggle outside, though it might only have been minutes. She had sat in the interim, listening to the silence, wondering.

The two men closed the bedroom door

behind them and stood just inside. The three of them stared at one another across the room, as if they were waiting for a formal introduction.

'She's a pretty little thing, ain't she?' the bearded man said finally.

'She is,' the other agreed, grinning even wider.

The man with the beard gestured with the knife and said, 'Take off your clothes.'

6

He crossed the room. One massive paw reached for Helen, was about to take hold of her, and stopped suddenly, frozen in midair. The man cocked his head to listen.

Helen heard it as well, pitched low at first, so that they had to make an effort to hear it. It seemed to steal through the house, like a ghost.

Helen was surprised. Without consciously thinking about it, she had supposed that both of her parents were dead by this time, and for a moment she could not think who this woman was who laughed so faintly. It was a funny kind of laugh, too, almost a snicker, and it seemed to drift about the house, moving disjointedly along the hall and into the room.

Helen saw now that the wolfish smile on the face of the man by the door faded. He turned toward the door and stared at it as if he expected that ghostly laugh to come through it in some palpable form.

The laughter stopped abruptly. It seemed to vibrate in the room after it had ended, though, and a moment later, it started up again. It was a roar of laughter now, the sound of hysteria, high, shrieking. You might have thought the woman was drunk, and enjoying some uproarious joke, she laughed with such unbridled energy.

Suddenly, there was a shout, and cries — screams, really.

When Helen had been a small child, her father had taken her to a food processing plant, and the pigs being driven down the chute into the big barn had screamed in much this way.

'Why are they screaming like that?' she had asked her father, and her father told her, in a matter-of-fact voice, 'They're being killed. The men inside are cutting their throats.'

Helen had not slept for nights after that, and she had never again been able to eat pork.

These screams were like that, shrill and chilling, and not quite human sounding.

They ended for a moment, and again there was that ponderous silence that seemed to weigh upon the three of them. Then, one more shriek, more horrible than the rest, and silence again.

They stood there, Helen and the two intruders, for what seemed an eternity, frozen in a tableau. Later, she realized that her mother's dying screams had saved her from whatever they had intended to do. But it hadn't felt at the time like she was being saved, somehow. It felt like . . . she couldn't say what. She refused to acknowledge the word that tried to slip into her mind: Disappointment.

In the next instant, pandemonium broke out. The front doorbell rang, following almost instantly by a loud pounding and shouts. In the hall outside the bedroom door, someone yelled, 'It's the pigs.' For a second or two, Helen actually thought they had shared with her that memory of the slaughterhouse, but they meant 'police.'

It was over as suddenly as it had begun. The two men ran from the bedroom with angry shouts, intent now on nothing but escape.

It turned out that there had been six young men in all. Two of them had escaped, but were captured shortly afterward. The others were arrested on the spot.

When the police came into Helen's bedroom, they found her dressed in her pajamas and wearing a bathrobe over them. She was seated primly at the window seat and she could not speak at all, not even to answer the simplest questions, not even to tell them her name.

Shock, it was decided, and she was taken to a hospital. Robbie found her there and moved her immediately to the Ville de Valle, where their mother had once been a patient for some weeks.

Helen had remained in carefully guarded seclusion there throughout the trial. Her presence as a witness was hardly needed. The intruders had been caught red-handed, both literally and figuratively. Their guilt was never in question, any more than was their fate.

Helen had never shared with anyone, not even Robbie, not even the doctors at the clinic, the details of that night. In truth, her own memories of them were blurred.

She recalled coming into the hallway in the company of a policeman. Through the open door, she could see the devastation in her father's bedroom, and she could see as well the trail of carnage that started in that room and went down the hall and descended the stairs, the blood a grisly testament to her father's struggle to escape.

Her father's body had been covered with a sheet, but as Helen and her accompanying police officer descended the stairs, someone chose that very moment to pull the sheet back, and she found herself staring down into her father's unseeing eyes.

Something odd happened to her then: it seemed as if she could see the entire struggle enacted before her eyes, as if she had been an eyewitness to it, had stumbled down the stairs along with her father.

Never, not if she lived to be a thousand years old, would she forget the expression on her father's face as he lay at the foot of the stairs, a look of such strength and of a will that it was determined to hold death at bay so long as it was possible.

There was more than that, though. He had come so close that perhaps he had actually believed that his escape was possible, but there was on his face when he died an expression of triumph.

It gave Helen the impression that her father had faced the angel of death, and stared him down.

7

'Miss Sparrow? Are you all right in there?'

It was Mrs. Hauptman's voice, quite real, just outside the bedroom door. Helen awoke with a start. Despite her fears, she had fallen asleep in the chair. Her limbs felt stiff and the back of her neck ached.

Her eyes went quickly around the room. Yes, it really was morning. Bright autumn sunlight poured through the window and there was nothing in the room with her to threaten or frighten.

'Yes, I'm fine, thank you,' she called back.

'It's after nine. I just wondered.'

'I'll be down in a minute.' Helen stretched her legs and kneaded the back of her neck. She got up from the chair and took the blanket back to the bed. For a moment she stared down at the spot where, the night before, she had dreamed she saw someone sit up. The sheet was wrinkled. Probably she had done that herself, tossing and turning. She laughed all of a sudden, actually giddy with relief that it was morning, the darkness gone, and everything after all just as it should be.

Her coffee was waiting when she came downstairs, and she was so grateful that she felt a sense of happy fellowship with her housekeeper, but when she greeted Mrs. Hauptman effusively, the woman only grunted and asked, 'Will you be having breakfast?'

'No, the coffee will be fine,' Helen said.

She went to the back door and opened it. It was a glorious day. The storm that had come up so suddenly during the night had vanished without trace. In the crisp morning air there was nothing at all ominous about the house. The house, she reminded herself, in which she had lived nearly all her life.

How silly she had been, all that melodrama of the night before. It was a good thing after all that there had been no one in the house with her to witness her foolishness. More than once, her father had warned her that her imagination was so overblown as to be a sin. Surely she had seen a good example of that herself last night.

Mrs. Hauptman came into the kitchen from cleaning elsewhere in the house, armed with brooms and cloths and spray bottles. She was a large and formidable woman, and Helen felt a pang of sympathy for any errant mote of dust that had fallen in her way.

'You're always up so early,' she said while she stowed things in the closet saved for cleaning supplies, 'I wondered if something had happened to you.'

'What could possibly happen to me?' Helen asked. 'I just overslept, is all. I sat up too late last night reading a book.'

She had no intention of sharing her bad dream with Mrs. Hauptman. She did not, in fact, feel entirely at ease with her. Which, she thought, was hardly surprising. She did not feel entirely at ease with herself.

Mrs. Hauptman went to the sink and began to fill it with soapy water. 'You had a restless night,' she said.

'Yes, I did,' Helen said a little warily, wondering how the housekeeper could have known that. Probably she had seen how disarrayed the bedclothes were.

'I hope you won't think it fresh of me to mention it,' Mrs. Hauptman said, busy now washing the dishes. 'It's your house, after all, and you can certainly sleep where you like, I'm sure. But I have to say, changing beds during the night, and every night too, does make for a bit of extra work on my part.'

Helen stared at her broad back, at the plump hands dipping in and out of the soapy water, and wondered what she could possibly mean.

'To be honest,' Mrs. Hauptman said, when Helen did not reply, 'I for the life of me can't imagine why you would want to sleep in those other rooms. After the things that happened in them, I mean to say. It seems, well, a bit odd, if you will forgive my saying so.'

'I hadn't actually thought of it that way,' Helen said, but the housekeeper's remarks made no sense to her. Since her return to the house, she had slept in her own bed, in her own room, every night. Where else would she sleep? And why?

She opened her mouth to say something, but Mrs. Hauptman looked over her shoulder then and paused in her dishwashing.

'I hope I haven't given offense,' she said. 'It's just that, if I am obliged to make up three beds every morning, instead of just the one, which is what I was expecting — well, you do see, don't you? It does cut back on the time I can spend on other things.'

'Of course, you're absolutely right,' Helen said. Satisfied that she had made her point, Mrs. Hauptman went back to her dishes.

Helen would like to have asked what three beds it was that she had been obliged to make up, but she could see that the question would sound peculiar. Obviously there had been extra beds to make, and Mrs. Hauptman thought she knew about them and to confess her ignorance could only make herself seem odd — or odder still. Under the circumstances, the last thing she wanted to do.

She finished her coffee instead, and even managed to linger over a second cup, before she left the housekeeper, now putting the dishes into the cupboard, and made her way slowly, thoughtfully, up the stairs.

She was sure that the door to her father's bedroom had been closed earlier, but it was open now. Of course, Mrs. Hauptman would have gone in there to dust. She skipped nothing in her regimen.

Her father's big old four-poster bed stood at the far end of the room. She went to it and stared down at it. It was neatly made. There was no way for her to tell if it had been disarranged earlier, or if it had been made up like this for months. Certainly it had been made up the day she had come home from the hospital, when she had looked in.

Or had it? She had not specifically looked at the bed, had she? Had come no further into the room than just inside the door.

And if it had been disturbed — even in her thoughts she could not say, 'slept in' — when had that happened? She could not possibly imagine anyone actually sleeping in that bed since her father's death.

It was Mrs. Hauptman who had straightened up the house when she had been informed that Helen was coming back to it. Perhaps she had simply overlooked the bed then, and forgotten it.

But she had been cleaning almost daily since then. Why had she not noticed it before? Or, perhaps she had and was only just now mentioning it.

Helen left the room and closed the door firmly after herself, and walked down the hallway to her mother's room. But again, just as before, she stopped outside the door. It was unreasonable, but she did not want to go in there, did not want even to see into that room. And why should she, she asked herself? Let the dead bury the dead.

And what if the bed in her mother's room was one of those Mrs. Hauptman had been obliged to make up this morning? The same explanation must apply, mustn't it? She had simply, for whatever reason, not made them up

79

before, when she was putting the house in order. They had just gone unnoticed until this morning and had given only an illusion of having been freshly disturbed.

It was peculiar, she knew, that so careful a housekeeper as Mrs. Hauptman should have been so careless in, not one, but two instances, and could have overlooked two unmade beds.

But there was no other explanation, was there? She was alone in the house. No one had come by to visit and most assuredly not to sleep overnight. There was nothing here but the unseen and unreal presence of memories from the past.

She frowned as she remembered her dream of the night before. But it had been only a dream. That was self-evident.

'Dreams do not disturb beds,' she told herself. 'Nor do memories.' For a moment after she had spoken, it seemed as if her words lingered on the air.

On the cold air, she thought, and shivered, because it was cold in this particular spot, outside the door to her dead mother's room.

When Mrs. Hauptman was preparing to leave for the day, Helen asked her about possibly working full-time.

'I know you said that you couldn't,' she said quickly, before the housekeeper could reply, 'but I thought maybe if I gave you a room of your own — or even a whole suite of rooms — you could stay over and wouldn't have to commute; and of course I'd pay you generously for the extra time and inconvenience.'

'And what about Mister Hauptman?' Mrs. Hauptman asked.

'Well, really, he could come here too, couldn't he?' Helen said, 'And think about it, it would save you the expense of keeping your own apartment.'

Mrs. Hauptman stood by the front door, her purse held protectively in front of her, and said, 'I hardly think Mister Hauptman would be agreeable to moving here. I can come mornings, and all day on Wednesday, if you'd like me to.'

'Yes, yes, I understand,' Helen said, talking faster now, 'but I just thought it would save you all that driving.'

'It would be much further for Mister Hauptman to drive to work.'

'And you'd save so much money. I wouldn't charge you any rent, of course; or anything, food or utilities.'

'If you're frightened about staying here alone . . . '

'I'm not frightened, Mrs. Hauptman, it's only . . . '

' . . . you should talk to your family — maybe one of them could stay with you. Or you could go stay with one of them. As I understand it, your Aunt Willa was against your coming back here at all, and to be perfectly frank, I myself can't think why you wanted to. She said . . . '

'I'm not afraid,' Helen said, more sharply than she had meant to.

Mrs. Hauptman pursed her lips disapprovingly. They stopped talking and looked coolly at one another for a long moment. Helen was breathing hard and she realized that she had let her composure slip. That was not a good thing, and especially not with a servant. She managed to laugh and shrugged her shoulders in a nonchalant fashion.

'There's nothing here to frighten me in this house,' she said. She made a broad gesture with her hands. 'For heaven's sake, this is my home. I lived my whole life here, and just because of, well, of that business that happened here, that was a long time ago, wasn't it, and it's hardly likely to happen a second time. I do hope you won't start telling people, people like Aunt Willa, that I'm frightened. Heaven only knows what they might think.'

Mrs. Hauptman continued to survey her sternly for another long moment. 'I can't come full-time,' she said finally, and went out, closing the door behind her with a loud bang.

The slam of the door seemed to echo through the hall, the sound of finality. Helen turned her back on the door, annoyed with the housekeeper for her stubbornness. It had been a perfectly good suggestion. It wasn't as if the Hauptmans lived in any kind of splendor. She had been to their apartment years ago with her father. It was a miniscule two-bedroom unit in a building that was not much more than a tenement, in a seedy part of town. And it wasn't as if they had children to think about, either; their two sons were both married and had moved away, far away. They were alone. All three of them were alone.

'It's ridiculous, really,' Helen said aloud, as if trying to convince the house, 'all of us living separately and alone, all that extra expense and housework, when they could just as easily share this big old house with me. Heaven knows, there's plenty of room and then some.'

She looked down the hall, toward the kitchen in the rear. In the morning, with the early sunlight, the house was almost cheery, but by now there were shadows forming and regrouping in the corners. She looked from one dim corner to another, and up the stairs, where the shadows seemed to thicken, and gave a small, dry laugh.

'Well, you can't make people have good sense, I suppose,' she said and shrugged again.

In the living room, she took up the book she'd selected the day before from the library and sat in a big overstuffed chair by one of the windows and tried to read, but her attention kept wandering from *The Decline and Fall of the Roman Empire*. No wonder it didn't hold her attention. Really, everything in the library was old and dull.

She made up her mind that she would buy some magazines later, maybe a thriller or two, or even a romantic novel. In the past, her father would never have allowed books like that in the house, although from time to time Robbie had smuggled something in. Once, she had even startled Helen with a magazine that had naked men in it. Helen remembered turning beet red when she saw the pictures, and quickly averting her eyes. Robbie teased her about it for weeks.

She wondered now where Robbie had gotten it. Surely you didn't just walk into a Barnes and Noble and pick something like that up; but she had no idea, though.

She put *The Decline and Fall* aside and got up, pacing the room briefly. There was a mirror over the mantel and, seeing herself in it, she thought that she looked wild-eyed, frenzied.

No wonder Mrs. Hauptman had looked at her so funny and thought she was scared. Her face was ghostly white and there were dark shadows under her eyes and her mouth was set in a tight, thin line.

'I look like I've been on a bender,' she said aloud. 'I don't look like myself'

When she thought about that, though, it occurred to her that she really did not know what 'myself' looked like. When you looked into a mirror, the features were so familiar that you hardly knew how someone else would see them. She studied her face critically, trying to imagine what a stranger would see.

All in all, she thought she looked insipid. There was nothing particularly distinguished about her features. Even her hair was a mousy brown. She wondered what she would look like if she bleached her hair the way Robbie had done. She had secretly always admired Robbie for having the courage to do that, although now that they were older, she could see that there was something a bit cheap about it. Which was exactly what their father had said, although Helen hated agreeing with her father about anything.

She stepped toward the mirror, trying to imagine what she would look like with blonde hair. There was a movement in the glass. Helen's eyes went wide and she put a hand on the mantel to support herself.

There was a man outside the French doors, on the terrace. He was only a blur through the curtains, but he was definitely there. Helen could see his outline as he leaned toward the window, as if he were trying to see into the room through the curtains.

The door handle rattled as he tried it. Helen stared at it. Had Mrs. Hauptman remembered to lock it? Surely she would not have left anything unlocked, not after what had happened.

Which was ridiculous, of course. A simple little bolt. Even a child, a strong child, could force that.

Just such illusory safety precautions had given them that false sense of security they'd had in the past. Just as one felt safe with a latched screen door in summer, when anyone could tear a screen door open. Safety, when you came down to it, was mostly psychological, wasn't it? An abstract idea that meant little in reality. Evil could come in anywhere, at any time.

It had here.

8

'Is anyone home?' a voice called from outside, and the handle on the French door rattled again. 'Mrs. Hauptman? Miss Sparrow?'

Helen let out the breath she had been holding. Not a prowler, then, but Mister Hoyle, the gardener and handyman who had always taken care of things for them. She should have realized, of course, that someone was keeping things up. The grass was freshly cut, wasn't it? Who else would that be but Mister Hoyle?

She went quickly to the French doors and unlatched them, swinging them wide to reveal Mister Hoyle standing there, his expression as stony as it had ever been. It was a measure of Helen's loneliness that she was so delighted to see the gardener.

She'd always thought him ugly and unfriendly; now, she had to restrain herself from embracing the squat old man staring at her. He wore loose trousers that seemed sizes too big for him and a dirty denim jacket, and his wrinkled face was the color of old leather.

'So, you are here,' Mister Hoyle said, and there was no trace of warmth either in his voice or his expression. 'I told Hauptman, that girl is crazy, coming back here. I said, what would she want to do that for? I thought maybe she was just pulling my leg, to tell you the truth.'

'It's good to see you, Mister Hoyle,' Helen said.

If he caught the note of sarcasm in Helen's voice Mister Hoyle didn't show it. 'I was just wondering as it's starting to get cool in the evenings,' he said. 'Do you want me to lay a fire in the fireplace? Your father liked to have a fire this time of year, when the nights starting cooling down.'

'Yes, that would be very welcome,' Helen said, trying to excuse his rudeness. 'Thank you for thinking of it.'

'Your father used to want one laid,' he said. He paused, turning his battered hat around in his hands.

'Please,' Helen said, and stepped aside.

Mister Hoyle came in, sidling past her as if afraid to make contact, and went directly to the fireplace.

'Funny thing,' he said, moving the fireplace screen carefully aside, 'I thought I saw him.' He bent down and brushed the back of his hand over the spotlessly clean hearth. Helen came to stand behind him and look over his shoulder. She might want to have a fire sometime in the future and it would be good to know how it was done.

'Saw who?' she asked Mister Hoyle's back.

'Your father. Just the other day. I was down at the far end of the yard, cutting the grass, and I happened to look up this way, and I'd have sworn I saw him standing at the back door watching me work, just the way he used to do. He always thought if he didn't keep an eye on me while I was working I'd figure some way to cheat him. I don't see how, cutting grass. It's either cut or it ain't, is how I see it.'

He chuckled at his own cleverness and there was a note of satisfaction — of triumph, almost — in his laugh; because, after all, he and his work had survived and the critical watcher hadn't.

'I'll just get some firewood from out back,' he said and started toward the French doors.

Helen shook her head, open-mouthed. 'But, it couldn't have been him,' she said.

He grunted. 'Course not, how could it be?' He gave Helen a look that said what he thought of that remark.

Helen dropped heavily into one of the armchairs that flanked the fireplace and stared after him. She had never liked Mister Hoyle, ever. The man had never treated her with any respect. Really, he had barely been civil most of the time, and many was the time she'd have complained to her father about him, if she hadn't been so afraid of her father. It was true, none of the servants had ever treated her with any particular respect, but Mister Hoyle had always been the worst. Mrs. Hauptman was polite, at least most of the time; you could say that much for her.

She had to give Mister Hoyle credit,

though, she thought with a sigh: he did take good care of things. You couldn't complain on that score.

Mister Hoyle came in through the French doors again, his arms filled with firewood. He carried it to the fireplace and dropped it noisily into the big bin there. One log rolled onto the carpet, but he left it where it fell. It occurred to Helen, she didn't even know where the firewood was kept. Mister Hoyle was already on his way back out.

'What did he do?' she asked, and jumped up to follow the gardener.

'Who?' Mister Hoyle asked without pausing.

'My father. The man you thought was my father, I mean.'

'Do? He didn't do anything. Just stood there and looked at me like your father used to, and when he saw me look at him, he just turned around and came back inside. What should he be doing?'

Helen followed him around the corner of the house. The door to the little wooden shed that stood there was open. Mister Hoyle went inside and emerged a moment later with another armload of wood, which he dropped onto the grass.

'But, who do you think it was?' Helen asked, trailing behind him back into the house.

'How should I know?' He began to rearrange the logs in the fireplace.

'But, if there is someone hanging around, I ought to know about it. Might it have been a prowler, do you think?'

He snorted his disdain at that idea. 'Hauptman had lots of men in and out getting the house ready. Delivery men, service people. The electric and the gas and all. It's a lot of work getting a place ready when it's been closed up for a while, you know. Takes as much work to do it for one person as for a whole family.'

He gave Helen an accusing look. 'I expect it was one of those I saw. It sure wasn't your father.'

'But you said . . . '

'I didn't say it was your father. I just said it looked like him. At the distance, and the way he was standing, and all. It was probably just a plumber, or the man to check the furnace. Excuse me. I got to lock the shed up.'

He started to go out again but he paused at the open door. 'There was some people down by the gate this morning. I had to chase them away.'

'What people?' Helen asked, surprised. Even before, when her father had been alive, there had rarely been anyone at the gate. They did not have many visitors. 'What did they want?'

'Come to stare, I expect,' he said, going out.

Helen did not follow him this time, only looked after him. She hadn't thought of that: sightseers, the morbidly curious. But they would be curious, of course, now that she thought about it. Before, most people had considered her a little strange; but now she was surely a genuine freak. Crazy Helen. And murder had been done. Not just your plain old garden variety of murder, either, but horrible, gruesome murder.

Add to that a trial, a public spectacle. Luckily, she had been shielded from most of it, at the Ville de Valle. The newspapers and magazines had been kept from her while the trial was taking place, so she had known almost nothing about it. Even the few times the police investigators had come to question her, the doctors had carefully supervised the sessions.

For which she had been grateful. She could tell the police almost nothing. Did tell them almost nothing, in any case, and the doctors had explained it carefully to the detectives: retrograde amnesia, her mind blocking out all memory of the trauma.

She had not testified at the trial, either, for the same reasons. She had told them all she could tell them, all she would tell them, in depositions. The doctors had seen to that.

And, really, what did it matter? There was never any question of the guilt of the young men who had done it, never any question how the trial would end. And it had ended just that way, with the convictions and the death sentences. Which, she had thought, surely was the end of it.

Shielded as she had been in the pink vacuum that was the Ville de Valle, her day-to-day existence so little disturbed by the events that transpired in the court-room, she'd had, really, no sense of how much stir it must have made. Robbie had told her, cautiously, that there had been some notoriety, but that had barely penetrated her consciousness.

She had scarcely realized that people would want to see where it had happened. Would want, most especially, to see who it had happened to. Who had survived the events of that grisly night.

Leaving the terrace, she crossed Mister Hoyle's neatly cut lawn to the front gate. At the moment there was no one there. She paused at the gate itself, one hand upon a wrought iron rung, and as she stood there, a car approached and slowed almost to a stop, the people inside the car staring shamelessly at her. The woman on the passenger's side in front leaned clear across the driver to get a better look, and an older woman in the rear lowered her window, the better to see.

'It's her,' she told the others, in something very near to a gleeful shout.

It did not even seem to discomfit them

that Helen saw them and stared back. She wanted to look away, or turn away, but she would not let herself.

Finally, the woman in front said something to the others that Helen could not hear and they all three laughed. The window went up again and the car moved off, gathering speed as it went, but the woman in the back seat turned to continue staring until they were out of sight.

Helen found herself unnerved by the experience. It was like being an animal in a zoo, behind iron bars, with people coming by to look. But what could she do about it? What did the animals in the zoo do?

She started back to the house, walking across the grass and through the little grove of maple trees. The leaves had mostly changed color by this time, red and brown and yellow. Everything was turning. It gave her a sense of finality. Life was terminal. Everything ended.

She saw some sort of seed pod on the ground and bent to pick it up. As she did, it burst in her hand, sending little tufts of seeds into the air. New life came out of death, but even in this resurrection there was no hope, was there? Life returned as itself, the plant became another plant just like the one that had died, not reborn into some higher, better existence, but locked into the same hopes, the same despairs. She wondered with real dread if she too would come back as well to the same dreary existence.

She turned the empty seed pod over in her fingers. If you looked at it just so, it was shaped almost like a penis. For some reason, she thought of her father.

She crushed it in her fingers and threw the pieces on the ground, and hurried toward the house.

★　★　★

I was alone. I was free, I had to answer to no one. I was aware of that almost from the first, but it was a trivial occurrence that actually brought that reality home to me. I was my own person now. Think what a revelation that was to me, of all people. Free.

Of course, I wasn't really free. I had merely traded masters. Who is truly free? Are you, Officer? Can you say or do whatever you like, without any concern for the consequences? Who can?

★ ★ ★

The ringing of the front doorbell so surprised her that it took a moment for its significance to register: she had a visitor. But no one had called on the little intercom at the front gate asking to be buzzed in. And the gate had been closed, hadn't it, when she had been there earlier? Of course, it probably wasn't locked. She hadn't even thought to check that. They had never locked it in the past.

'I should see that it's locked,' she thought as she went to answer the door. But, really, that was like the bolt on the French windows, wasn't it? Those men had climbed over the wall on that fateful night, but the gate had been unlocked then, too. Had they only known, they could simply have opened it and walked through. What difference would it have made? The end result would have been the same.

It was Reverend Williams from the Baptist church her father used to attend. 'I'm sorry,' he apologized when Helen opened the door, 'I rang and rang the bell at the front gate and nobody answered, so I just let myself in and came up.' He was a tall, thin man with a prominent nose and a bald head.

'It must not be working,' Helen said. 'Maybe it's disconnected. I'll ask Mister Hoyle to look at it. Come in, please, why don't you?'

Her father had always entertained the minister in his library, and this was where Helen took him now. It was not a room with which she was particularly familiar and one in which she invariably felt uncomfortable. She had not been permitted to come in here when she'd been a child, as it had been her father's private preserve, and she still felt unwelcome, as if the room resented her intrusion.

'Please, sit down,' she invited the reverend. 'Would you like some coffee? Or a drink, perhaps?'

'I'm not a drinking man,' the reverend said sternly; but immediately his expression softened a bit and he added, 'but your father did use to pour me a glass of his elderberry wine, if you still have that.'

Helen found that in the liquor cabinet, labeled in her father's bold and unfaltering hand, and poured a small glass for the reverend. She would have liked to have a glass herself, more out of curiosity than anything else, since she had never tasted it, but she was not sure that would be appropriate.

She sat in a chair facing the minister and watched him take a tentative sip of the wine. 'Ah, yes, just as I remembered,' he said, licking his lips. He turned his attention from the wine to Helen. 'It's good to see you,' he said. 'And at home, too.' He smiled and leaned back in his chair, taking another sip of the wine.

'I'm glad to be home,' Helen said, a little tentatively. She thought that the reverend had the air of a man who had something on his mind more than just welcoming her home, but she could not think what that could possibly be.

'You've been through a difficult time,' the reverend said. Helen thought that needed nothing more from her than a nod. 'But though we may think of afflictions as birds of ill omen, spiritually they are like the ravens, are they not, who fed the prophet? And it may be that when those afflictions visit the faithful, they bring nourishment for the soul.'

'Perhaps,' Helen said cautiously. She could not imagine in what way her experiences of the last few years could have benefited her soul but she did not want to say this to the reverend. She smiled faintly and watched the minister swirl the purple liquid about in his glass.

'I am certain that your dear departed father would have wished that you would be spiritually stronger for what happened to him. And to you, too, of course.' He followed the direction of Helen's eyes, and seemed suddenly fascinated by the eddy of the wine in his glass.

There was a brief silence between them. Helen could not think what she ought to say, and waited for the reverend to speak instead.

After a moment, Reverend Williams stirred himself and said, 'Your father was a deeply religious man.'

Helen was tempted to say that she thought her father had acquired religious scruples only after he had gotten everything else that he wanted. She felt no bitterness over this. She thought that people were idiotic to suppose that a wise and powerful God would have chosen this foolish man sitting before her as his representative on earth. Any earthbound government would have chosen a better ambassador, surely.

'And he was, in every way, a pillar of support for the church,' the reverend added, in a voice so soft it was almost a whisper. 'Not only in the money he gave, though of course he was quite generous with that, but more importantly, he was a pillar of moral support.'

Helen suddenly understood. She had only superficially grasped something of which she had earlier been informed: the money was hers. Not only was she free of her father, but she was now the mistress of this house, the heir to her father's considerable wealth.

She had only a vague idea how considerable. All of that was handled by the lawyers and accountants who had managed it before, and Helen was quite content to let them do so. But, of course, charitable donations would depend on instructions from her. As, surely, they had depended before upon her father.

'Oh,' she said, surprised by the realization, and she sat forward abruptly in her chair.

Her sudden movement startled the reverend, who, thinking he might have given offense, set his glass down on the little table next to his chair and leaned sharply forward as well, so that the two of them looked as if they were literally putting their heads together to share some secret.

To the reverend's great relief, however, Helen quickly recovered herself. She smiled brightly and said, 'And I will want to continue his generosity, of course, Reverend.'

This announcement left Reverend Williams noticeably relieved. He picked up his glass again and this time drained it. 'Well,' he said, smacking his lips noisily, 'I won't keep you, I know that you must still be very tired. I merely wanted to welcome you home. And if there is ever anything you need me for, I assure you I am at your disposal. Of course, there is always a friend who is even closer at hand.'

Helen's thoughts had drifted, but she brought herself back to the moment and asked, absentmindedly, 'And who is that?'

The Reverend drew back slightly as if offended. 'I refer to our Good Lord, of course.'

'Oh, of course,' Helen said, blushing. 'I'm afraid my thoughts were elsewhere for a moment.'

'Yes. I can see that.' The reverend stood.

Helen accompanied him to the front door, but when they were there, the door open, she asked, 'Reverend, do you think there is something that lingers when people die?'

'Lingers?' he asked, looking uncertain.

'Of the spirit, I mean.'

'Oh, yes, of course.' The reverend

nodded his head, brightening. 'You must remember, the spirit is immortal. The flesh profits nothing, but the spirits surround us at all times, wherever we are. Swedenborg put it nicely, I think, when he said that even when we think that we are wrapped in darkness and alone, we stand in the center of a great theater.'

He made to leave, but paused again. 'That theater is as wide as the starry chamber of heaven, and the audience sees you as if you were under a flood of light, an audience so vast that no man can count its numbers. Even when you think that you are in darkness, you are in light, you are surrounded by witnesses. But he who loves corruption shall have enough of it.'

He extended his hand to Helen. 'Goodbye, now. I will come again to see you, when you will be more yourself, I am sure, and at that time we can discuss what role you plan to play in the church. Please give my blessings as well to your dear sister. Though she has strayed, she remains in our prayers.'

When he had gone, Helen thought

about his remark that Robbie had strayed. Simply by escaping their home and their father's tyranny?

But her thoughts quickly came back to her remarkable realization: she was her father's heir. She had inherited everything. She couldn't imagine now why that truth had not fully registered with her before. For the first time in her life, she was dependent upon no one for anything. It was astonishing to grasp that fact.

But another, sobering, thought followed quickly on the heels of that one: there were other relatives. Robbie, of course, had gotten nothing, but the others had received only token inheritances. Which no doubt did much to explain why they were cool to her; antagonistic, even.

And which only emphasized what Robbie had warned her of: those relatives would have preferred that she be committed permanently; not at Ville de Valle, which was too discreet for their purposes, but at an honest-to-goodness insane asylum, a state-run one perhaps. In that case, they would certainly be able to gain full control of the money.

There was no doubt that they would do just that, given the opportunity. In that sense, she was not after all so free or independent as she had imagined herself. She was at the mercy of the rest of the family, dependent upon their judgment for her freedom. She must guard her every word and deed, lest she give them an excuse to do what they surely wanted to do.

She had known all of this since she had left Ville de Valle, but it was not until her conversation with Reverend Williams that it had truly come home to her.

Her father had come late but in full fever to a harsh brand of religion that would have done Knox or Helen proud.

'I won't have you behaving like other children,' he had said more than once, and he had certainly made that true. But although he rigidly disapproved of certain kinds of behavior, such as drinking, his taboos were meant to apply mostly to others. He had made his own private pact with God as to what was permitted and what was not. He had often spoken of God as if the two of them were in the habit of talking things over after dinner with a glass of port and a good cigar. It was clear that he regarded God as king, but it was equally clear that he considered himself the power behind the throne.

No doubt, Helen thought wryly, in the evil that had befallen him, it was God who had failed in his duties.

The afternoon was growing late, the shadows in the house gathering and thickening in that odd way they had. Mrs. Hauptman had left some cold roast chicken for her in the kitchen. She made herself a sandwich and drank some lemonade with it for her dinner.

By the time she had eaten and put things away it was evening. She turned on lights as she came back into the living room. It occurred to her that there was hardly a corner of the room that did not remain in shadow, notwithstanding that she turned on all of the lamps. She decided she would spend some of her new wealth to have the house rewired, perhaps even have fluorescent lighting installed, the sort that had been concealed in the ceilings at Ville de Valle.

She remembered the fire that Mister Hoyle had laid for her in the fireplace, and she lit that. For some reason she felt gloomy, and she thought that maybe the fire would cheer her.

It did not, however. The flames, dancing and crackling, only seemed to bring the darkness in the far reaches of the room to an eerie life of their own. Glancing from the corner of her eye, she almost thought she saw the shadows move, take shape. More than once she was sure she had detected some movement, and looked quickly in that direction, but it was nothing, only the shadows, shifting in the firelight, making the empty room seem crowded.

Reverend Williams' words came back to her, of spirits that watched her endlessly, crowding about her. At the time she had thought his remarks silly, but now they took on a different significance. She could almost sense those spirits hovering, watching her every movement.

Impatient with herself she went back to the kitchen for a glass of warm milk. Something, some sound and yet not quite sound, seemed to go down the hall before her. It was unnerving, and she found herself more on edge than ever. She passed through the darkness of the dining room and suddenly found herself facing someone else, another face as startled and frightened as her own, and she gasped aloud.

It was only her own reflection in the mirror. There were mirrors on each of the four walls, and as she paused to look into the one before her, she saw a crowd of strangers watching, strangers who turned out to be only herself, multiplied over and over. She hurried past their anxious, watching eyes into the kitchen, but they were waiting for her when she came back through the room, and every one of them at whom she glanced was glancing back at her as well.

She was almost grateful to be back with the dancing shadows surrounding the fireplace.

9

Have you ever had a dream in which you see someone, someone you know, but you cannot identify him; and the face is smiling, cheerful really, and yet for some reason, you do not know why, you are frightened by it? And when you wake, you know that you were frightened, and the fear lingers after the dream, but you cannot say why you were frightened or what caused you the fear?

That is how it was for me during this period of time in the house. I was in my own home, in which I had lived all but the last few years of my life. I was intimately acquainted with those shadows, I knew every groan and every creak of rafter or floorboard or stair. I could have put a name to that rustle of the curtains in the breeze, and called it by that name ever after.

I was frightened, though, and I did not know why, or what frightened me.

Has anything like this ever happened to you? Have you looked at someone whom you knew, a friend perhaps, or even a loved one, and fleetingly you seemed to see something, something you cannot even name, but that is different, from what you expected to see, and that disconcerted you, that gave you an inexplicable chill? Have you ever, for just that fraction of a second, thought that this individual hated you, wanted to do you harm? Have you ever experienced a reasonless terror just from stepping into a familiar room? Has your blood ever run cold when you encountered something that you knew was dull and commonplace?

That is what it was like for me in that house.

★　★　★

At last, her nerves utterly undone, Helen decided she could bear no more. Despite the fact that it was only eight o'clock in the evening, she gave up her pretense of reading and, putting the screen before the still burning fire on the hearth, she went upstairs. It seemed to her as she came into her bedroom that it was particularly cold.

She was no more relaxed here, though, than she had been downstairs. All of her tension, all those nagging fears and anxieties, assailed her. She tried to make her mind clear, to rid it of all thoughts, but she would drift just to the very edge of sleep, and then something, some sound, some alarm, would jerk her back, her eyes flying open.

She sat up in bed, clutching the bed-clothes, her gaze darting about the room, seeking an intruder. It was useless to reason with herself then; all of the reason in the universe could not still her pounding heart.

Again, she concentrated on peaceful things, harmless and gentle things. She counted sheep, and daisies, and she recited to herself one of her favorite poems, 'How Do I Love Thee?'

She was in misery. She could have cried with frustration. And then, when she had finally given up all hope of ever falling asleep and had decided that she might as well after all go back downstairs for her book and read for a bit, she fell asleep at last.

This was not Shakespeare's gentle, restorative sleep, however, but as filled with phantoms and unnamed terrors as her waking had been. Voices whispered to her, the shadows lurked and leered. Every unpleasant experience of her childhood came to visit her, with all the terror to which childhood is prey. Every nightmare she had ever suffered was played anew on the screen of her mind.

When she felt her father's hand on her shoulder, shaking her awake, she could only feel a sense of relief. She was grateful to escape this torture of dreams, regardless of how early it was.

It was early, too. When she opened her eyes, the room was still dark, the light of the full moon outside the window turning everything to pewter and silver.

Her father had stopped shaking her, but she could still feel the warmth and the weight of the hand on her shoulder. But why was he waking her so early? She blinked and rolled onto her back — and remembered, like a slap on the face: her father was dead. That hand, gone now, could not have been his.

There was no one there. The room was empty.

She sat up with a gasp, almost crying with alarm, her shoulders shaking convulsively, and looked frantically around the room. But there really was no one to be seen. She sat without moving for a long moment, staring, waiting for someone to step out of the deep shadows there by the closet, but nothing moved. The house seemed to be holding its breath with hers.

She could not help remembering that other night. The horror had begun with a hand shaking her awake. She had thought then, too, that it was her father. Somehow, she was reliving the nightmare of that experience.

Trembling violently, she scrambled from her bed. She turned on all of the lights and hurried to the closet, and snatched a robe from within it, without daring to glance inside. She left her room and hurried downstairs, all but running past the open door to her father's bedroom. Hadn't it been closed earlier? She hadn't the courage to look inside that room. She turned on every light as she went.

The kitchen lights were the brightest in the house. When she turned them on, the glare hurt her eyes, but it sobered her some too. She put the teakettle on the stove. There was a bolt on the door from the hallway, and she closed the door and threw the bolt, and went to the outside door and checked that lock as well, to be sure it was secured.

When the kettle began to whistle, she made herself a full pot of tea, dark and so strong that it was bitter to the taste, and took it with her to the oilcloth-covered table against the wall.

That was where she spent the rest of the night, sipping tea at the little table in the over-bright kitchen. Once, she thought she heard something in the hall outside. She was sure she could hear someone breathing on the other side of the door, and she stared at the doorknob, expecting it to turn, but it did not.

Nothing happened. No one came until she heard Mrs. Hauptman's heavy tread as she came in the front door in the morning and started down the hall.

'Mrs. Hauptman?' she called, to be sure. 'Good morning.'

'Good morning,' Mrs. Hauptman called back. Helen heard the rustle of her coat as she hung it on the coat tree. 'You're up early.'

She got up quickly and slid the bolt back so Mrs. Hauptman would not question why she had locked herself in the kitchen.

* * *

It had begun to rain, lightly at first and then harder. The raindrops against the window panes sounded to Helen like someone tapping at them, and the rush of the wind about the corners of the house was like a chorus of voices calling some indistinguishable warning.

She had to get out of the house, weather or no weather. She felt as if the house were mocking her, jeering at the terror she had suffered. The walls closed in upon her until she thought that she would suffocate. She could not bear to listen to any more of Mrs. Hauptman's fragmentary conversation.

'You're not going out in this weather, are you?' the housekeeper asked when Helen put on her raincoat. 'It's ugly out there.'

'It won't bother me,' Helen said, finding an old canvas hat of her father's and setting that on her head. It was too windy for an umbrella but she donned a raincoat. 'All that time being shut up, it's nice to think that I can just go out when I want. I'll be glad to have some rain in my face.'

She did not add that she thought it was uglier inside than out. The gloomy day only made the shadows inside gloomier too, darker than ever. They writhed and swirled just out of her sight, and when she looked at them directly, they subsided into a waiting stillness.

'It won't just be in your face,' Mrs. Hauptman said darkly. 'You'll be soaked in no time.'

When Helen let herself out the front door, the wind tried to push her back inside, as if conspiring with the house, but she went determinedly down the front steps, glad to be outside despite the weather. The rain blew into her face, but it helped to restore her consciousness, washing away the lingering cobwebs.

It was no more than a mile or two to the cemetery. She went past a flower shop just outside its gates and, finding it open, went in and bought a large mixed bouquet.

The cemetery was the oldest in town. Originally it must have stood off entirely by itself, but the town had spread since then, and now there were houses surrounding it, and shops; and directly across from the ornate gate, standing open, a coffee house with a neon sign that looked particularly ill-suited.

She knew the exact path to her parents' graves. They rested beside one another. Doctor Martin himself had accompanied her to their funeral, and a large band of the clinic's staff had been with them as well, to keep the curious and the press away from her. It was no particular kindness, she knew that. The fees that Ville de Valle charged were certainly enough that they could afford that sort of personal attention.

The funeral had taken place in the afternoon, in the chilled interior of the church, and the graveside ceremony in the shadow of the gray and antiquated church tower. It had been winter, a bleak and cheerless day, and snow began to fall while they were at the graveside. Helen remembered being mesmerized by the large flakes settling upon the two mahogany coffins, the white of the snow in startling contrast to the dark wood.

Something had gone wrong with the mechanism that lowered the caskets into the ground, and her father's coffin moved only a few inches and stuck. There had been a hasty conference to decide whether to leave it as it was and go ahead with the ceremony, or whether to call someone in to fix it. The others of the family had all been for finishing the ceremony with the coffin above ground, but Helen had insisted that the mechanism be repaired and the coffin lowered into the ground.

She had offered no explanation for her insistence, but she had been adamant despite all arguments and cajoling, and in the end, she had her way. She had the impression that her father was still struggling against death and refused to be put away, and she had been convinced that if he did not go into the ground now, he would never be put to rest.

It had taken the better part of an hour to have the problem fixed. It was cold. The funeral party waited in sullen silence, stamping their feet and rubbing their hands, and pretending not to notice the workmen who handled the coffin in a matter-of-fact manner.

Helen had spoken to no one during this interim. She watched the snowflakes fall and melt upon the coffins, like heavenly tears. She could not remember that she had ever seen her parents remain so close to one another for so long. Perhaps it was this that her father resisted.

Later, when the funeral was over and she was back within the pink walls of Ville de Valle, she had a feeling of dissatisfaction. She had a strange impression that she and her father were not yet done with one another, and she had come very close to asking Doctor Martin if she could return to the cemetery just once. She wanted to assure herself that her father was still there, that the grave was undisturbed.

She had not asked, though. The suspicion in which she was held meant that there were many things she could not do that she would have liked to do. People suspected she was insane.

It would not take much to convince them, she was sure.

* * *

Because, if they once get it into their heads that you are crazy, they never stop watching you, weighing your every word and action. The truth is, you can never again act normally, because what is normal for others becomes unacceptable in your case.

People act crazy, normal people, don't you agree? They do irrational things for no good reason, they lose their tempers and swear at others, they act out of spite and do mean things, or they get frightened. Everyone does. They can spill a drink and no one *thinks* anything of it, or *forget* someone's name, or a word they're searching for. Normal people get confused, or they change their minds at will, a hundred times a day perhaps, or decide they don't want to eat something just because they don't feel like it, or decide to try something they never ate before. They can be upset and throw a book on the floor, violently even. Or think they hear something at night. Have you never imagined you heard someone downstairs, and wondered if it were only your imagination, or a prowler?

When you are considered normal, people take your actions for normal; but if they think for a moment that you're crazy, every thing and anything that you do can be seen as a sign of that.

* * *

She didn't know how long she had been standing at her parents' graves. Only she became aware that someone was watching her. At Ville de Valle, she had become supernaturally tuned to the awareness of

125

people watching her. She looked around. For one awful moment she half-expected to see her parents standing behind her, her father scowling his disapproval.

It was only a caretaker, though, preparing a gravesite a short distance away. He gave Helen a curious glance. Probably he was wondering why someone should even be here on a day like this, should stand so long in the pouring rain.

Helen divided up the flowers. The white carnations she laid on her mother's grave, and the big yellow daisies on her father's. She had roses too, pink ones, but they felt too velvety, looked too seductive, for either grave.

In the end, she took them with her when she started for home. It was still raining hard and there were not many people abroad, but she passed two women at different times. Both of them stared at her from under their umbrellas. She had no doubt she looked peculiar, her arms full of roses, walking in the downpour without an umbrella. Despite her coat and the canvas hat, she was soaked through.

Yet though the women looked at her as she passed by them in the opposite direction, she had a strange sense that they did not actually see her. Hers was the invisibility of alienation, the isolation of people one from another.

She walked past the walls that surrounded her home. Those walls had not kept out the young men who had come that night to kill. Walls could be climbed easily — walls like this, in any case.

There were other walls, though. She had passed within inches of other people this day, but there was a wall that had separated her from them, and it was insurmountable. She had no hope that she could ever cross that phantom wall. But she did not know if the wall was within her, or within them.

She knew that she was different from other people. She had lived all her life in this wretched isolation, and though she had dreamed of what it would be like to have friends, as other people did, she knew that the gap between those dreams and their fulfillment was unbridgeable. She would never know what others knew about friendship, about love, about ordinary human relations.

She reached the gates and paused, one hand on the iron railings, to look up at the house in the distance, blurred now in mist and rain. It seemed to be waiting for her return. *What is it that you want of me?* she asked. *I know you are there, I can feel you, watching, waiting* — but for what?

If only she knew how to climb that wall.

10

She saw, as she came up the driveway, that there was a car parked there, a big silver Mercedes. She recognized it as Aunt Willa's. She was not particularly eager to see her and avoided the front door, circling instead to the terrace and entering through the French doors.

She had been walking in the rain and she knew she looked dreadful, but that was not her real reason for delaying the meeting with Aunt Willa. Her aunt frightened her. She knew that this visit was not occasioned by any affection or concern. Aunt Willa was one of those who would rather have her certified as insane and committed to a real asylum.

The truth was, she supposed, that Aunt Willa would have preferred to have her dead. Which was to say, Aunt Willa was 'the enemy.'

There was no one in the living room when she came in. She draped her wet raincoat across the back of a chair so it would drip on the hearth rather than the carpet, and left the canvas hat on the terrace outside. It could hardly get any wetter.

She was still carrying the pink roses. The rain actually seemed to have refreshed them, and even here their vibrant warmth seemed out of place. She found a vase in the china cabinet and put the flowers in it, and set them outside too, so the rain would fill the vase.

After that, she stole quickly upstairs, grateful that the hall was empty. Presumably Aunt Willa and Mrs. Hauptman were in the kitchen. In her room, she shed her wet clothes and left them in the bathroom, and donned a dry housedress and combed her hair, so that she did not look quite so much like a drowned rat.

Her aunt was aggressively chic, always perfectly coiffed and made up, and dressed in the best styles. Helen had always felt even more mousy than usual when Aunt Willa was around. People thought Aunt Willa attractive. To the best of her knowledge, no one had ever thought that of her. No one, that was to say, but those men who had come to her room on that fateful night.

When she came down, she found Aunt Willa coming along the hall. 'My goodness, there you are,' her aunt greeted her. 'I was wondering what had happened to you. When did you come in?'

'Just a few minutes ago,' Helen said. 'I was rather soaked. I went up to change and dry myself off.'

She paused on the stairs to look down at the tall, slim woman below. Aunt Willa was wearing the sort of tailored black pantsuit that could have looked severe on someone else, but seemed the epitome of elegance on her. Her hair, on this occasion, was a pale yellow, almost silver. She moved, as she did everything, with a studied grace, and it was impossible to say how old she was.

'She sheds the years as easily as the husbands,' Robbie had once said of her.

'I didn't hear you come in,' Aunt Willa said. The tone of her voice and the way she looked up at Helen made an indictment out of it. 'Well,' she said after getting no reply, 'I've come down to spend the night. I have to be back in Boston tomorrow, but I wanted to see how you are doing.'

'That's kind of you,' Helen said. 'I'm fine. Really, just fine. To be honest, I was fine most of the time I was at . . . when I was away. I just needed the rest, and the time to recover.'

'And have you?' Aunt Willa's gaze was shrewd, weighing. 'Recovered, I mean? Truly?'

'Yes. Truly.'

Aunt Willa had not visited her once while she was at the clinic, nor even written. Her sudden interest in her niece's wellbeing was a bit transparent.

As if Helen had spoken aloud, Aunt Willa said, 'I meant to come visit you while you were there, but I couldn't get away. You've no idea what can go on during a divorce proceeding. You'd think by this time I would have the process perfected, wouldn't you?'

She laughed, but when Helen did not join in, she let her laugh fade away. 'Well, there's no reason for you just to stand there on the stairs staring at me,' she said, sounding a bit peevish. 'I'm not going to bite you.'

'Of course not,' Helen said, but with no real conviction. 'Have you had lunch?'

'Hauptman is fixing some now. I was just about to make myself a martini. You'll have one with me, won't you?'

She led the way into the living room. A stranger, seeing them, would have supposed it was Aunt Willa who lived here; and Helen, trailing meekly after her, who was the guest.

'Good heavens, who put those roses out in the rain? I'm sure they weren't there a few minutes ago.'

'I left them out there to collect some water,' Helen said. 'I bought them for the cemetery, but they didn't seem quite right there, so I brought them home with me.'

'I can't imagine why you would think they were right here, either. I mean, really, Helen, dead roses? It seems a bit morbid to me, if you don't mind my saying so.'

'Dead?'

She looked. The roses were indeed

dead. The limp stems drooped over the sides of the vase, and the blooms, what was left of them, looked as if they were weeks old. Petals had fallen onto the tiles of the terrace.

'They were so fresh when I brought them home,' she said. 'I suppose they needed more water than they got from the rain.'

Her aunt looked at her strangely. 'Oh, well,' she said, 'it's nothing to be upset about. A few dead roses.'

'I'm not upset,' Helen said, rather too quickly.

'It's not good for you to get yourself all worked up, you know.' Aunt Willa crossed to the liquor cabinet and began to make drinks. 'Over a few flowers. Some dead roses.'

'I'm not upset,' Helen said again.

It was no use. She had never been able to have any kind of real conversation with her aunt. Her father had said his sister was crazy, but probably no one had ever tried to have her committed.

Aunt Willa handed her a martini in a stemmed glass. 'Now,' she said, and seated herself in the chair that had always been Helen's father's, the chair no one else had ever dared to sit in, 'tell me, darling, how are you, really? You look drawn. Did they treat you properly at that place?'

'Ville de Valle? Yes, they treated me very nicely.'

Aunt Willa waited, seemingly expecting more. When it was not forthcoming, she said, 'Well, I should hope they would. It certainly cost enough. I said to Robbie, I can't imagine how any hospital could justify that sort of money. And not a real hospital, either. Just a clinic.'

'Yes. A psychiatric clinic,' Helen said. She wanted to add, *It is my money*, but she did not. She took a sip of her drink instead. She did not really like the medicinal taste of martinis, but no doubt if she declined to drink one, Aunt Willa would see that too as evidence of her mental imbalance.

The conversation seemed to have died. Aunt Willa tried to revive it, bringing up a variety of subjects, but they really had no common ground. The things that interested one did not interest the other.

Helen had no knowledge of, nor interest in, the latest gossip from the society columns, and she knew even less about the latest fashions. She had never been to a Broadway show, nor eaten at those elegant restaurants around the world of which Aunt Willa liked to boast. And what could Helen have contributed to a discussion on romance, when she had never known one?

Still, Aunt Willa continued introducing subjects, her remarks met more often than not by monosyllables. She found herself reflecting once again upon what a peculiar person her niece was. She always had been.

★ ★ ★

The afternoon and evening were uncomfortable for both of them. They were not suited to sharing one another's company under the best of circumstances, and Helen could hardly be unaware that she was being weighed in the balance. And surely being found wanting.

Even Mrs. Hauptman seemed to be

siding with Aunt Willa against her. More than once she saw them exchange glances with one another, glances that seemed filled with meaning.

The two women had been alone in the house while she had been at the cemetery. Almost certainly they had discussed her. Aunt Willa would have been eager to question the housekeeper about her, and Helen could imagine the kinds of things Mrs. Hauptman might have said:

'She changes beds during the night. I come in the mornings and the beds are messed up in the other rooms. And I don't care what she says, she's afraid of staying here alone. She tried to convince me to come and stay. She even went so far as to suggest that Mister Hauptman and I both come, that we move right in here with her. Of course I said no.'

Helen could all but hear Mrs. Hauptman's emphatic voice as she delivered these bits of gossip. For the first time it occurred to her that maybe Hauptman was keeping an eye on her. Maybe the family had instructed the housekeeper to watch her behavior, and report to them.

Once, during the early evening, Aunt Willa went to the kitchen. Helen had been pretending to read, but she found herself staring down the hallway after her, wondering just what errand had taken her aunt there. She imagined the two women alone in the kitchen together, talking about her again, comparing notes.

'She doesn't act right, you can see that for yourself.' Helen could easily imagine the housekeeper saying those very words.

'I've tried all day to make some kind of conversation with her, but she knows nothing at all about anything going on in the world,' Aunt Willa could say in return. 'It's like she lives in some place of her own.'

Helen wondered what they actually were saying. What could the two of them have to discuss, if not her? Aunt Willa was only here for the night; she would be leaving in the morning. It wasn't as if she needed to discuss the scheduling of household chores with the housekeeper.

Helen's uneasiness grew with the passing of the minutes, became down-right aggravation. It wasn't right that she should be subject to this snooping. Aunt Willa was a guest. Her guest. If she chose, she could march out to the kitchen this very moment and demand that Aunt Willa leave at once. She would be perfectly within her rights. Anyone could see that.

Finally, in exasperation, she tossed aside the magazine she had been reading and went purposefully toward the kitchen. The kitchen door was closed, though. She stopped outside it. She could hear them beyond the door, speaking in a low murmur, like conspirators.

She put her ear to the door, but could make out no more than an occasional word or two. If only they would speak in their normal voices, or if the door were not so thick . . .

It was ridiculous, having to spy on them like this, her aunt and her housekeeper, in her own home. She had half a mind to barge into the room and tell them what she thought of the whole affair.

She really wanted to know, though, what they were saying. She got on her knees, putting her eye to the keyhole, but she could see nothing but Hauptman's thick hips and a bit of her apron. She heard her say, 'can't eat butter . . . ' but she had no idea what that meant. She had no problem with eating butter, and who else would they have been talking about?

Hauptman was a fool, siding like this with Aunt Willa, who would never do anything for her. If she got the money, if Helen were placed in an asylum, Hauptman would get nothing for her efforts. Aunt Willa had never done anything for anyone else, except make trouble.

And you, she thought, addressing her aunt silently, *you should have been here that night, you should have been the one hacked and beaten and shot. It should have been your rich blood spilled along the hallway and down the stairs.*

And if you try to take me away from here, dear Aunt . . .

'Helen? What on earth?'

The unexpected swing of the kitchen door had knocked Helen on her rump on the dining room floor. Aunt Willa stood in the doorway, staring down at her in astonishment.

'What are you doing on the dining-room floor?' she asked. 'Why were you stooped by the door?'

'I . . . ' Helen was dazed. She shook her head. 'I was looking for something.'

But in truth, she did not know why she had been on her hands and knees outside the kitchen door. She remembered coming here, but vaguely, as if it were something she had done a long, long time ago, or maybe something in a dream.

Her head hurt, and there was some thought that hovered just out of conscious reach, like a name on the tip of one's tongue that can't quite be remembered.

11

There were no fairy tales in our library when I was a little girl, Officer Wallace, no Cinderella or Sleeping Beauty or Peter Pan. I had to read what was there, or not at all. So I read Schopenhauer.

Schopenhauer says that there is no such thing as free will, neither, in the philosopher who throws a stone nor in the stone itself, although both of them believe otherwise. The stone thinks, as it sails through the air, that its will is free, but it is only an illusion. Everyone likes to believe that he is free in his individual actions, that at any point in time he can change his life and begin another one, or become another person altogether.

But though a man thinks about change, he does not change. Necessity rules him, often necessity of which he is unaware. From beginning to end, he acts out his assigned role.

We do not exercise Will. Will is the

hand the throws the stone. It directs us. We are imprisoned in a life that is worse than hell. How did Dante fashion his hell, after all? Everything that he wrote, everything that he portrayed, came from the world of man.

What a rich wealth of material he had to choose from, don't you think?

★ ★ ★

There was a full moon. Not, she supposed, *the* full moon. That was for just one night, wasn't it? Last night. And by tomorrow night, it would have lost some of its roundness, would already be seen to shrink.

But for tonight, to her amateur's eye, it looked just as full as it had the night before. She stood at the window in her bedroom and looked at the silvery world outside. It had been just such a night as this, a night of a full moon, when it had happened.

Was it nothing more than coincidence that had brought Aunt Willa to stay this particular night?

'Are you sure you wouldn't like me to sleep in your room, in the other bed?' Aunt Willa had asked. 'Wouldn't you sleep better?'

'No thank you, Aunt,' she had replied, and added, 'I sleep quite well, actually.' She did not add that whatever happened, it would happen to her alone; she would not share it, however unpleasant the experience, not with Aunt Willa.

Anyway, she knew perfectly well she wouldn't sleep a wink, knowing Aunt Willa was there, watching her, watching to see . . . but to see what? What did she expect? To see her niece sleepwalking? Or performing some eerie midnight ritual, evidence at last of real lunacy?

Lunacy. The word stuck in her mind. From the ancient word for the moon, Luna. Maybe those ancients had been right, blaming the moon for madness. Maybe people did go moon-crazy.

She fell asleep in bed with thoughts like those swirling through her mind.

She did not know exactly when she stopped sleeping and when she knew that she was awake, listening to something that was real and not just a part of her dreams.

She was quite sure, though, that she did not want to be awake, did not want to know that she was hearing those sounds and not dreaming them: the low, laughing sounds that belonged in dreams, in nightmares really.

A woman's voice. A near-laugh, actually, more of a chuckle. It crept through the house ghostlike, moved down the hall outside, and slipped like mist into her bedroom.

She had heard this before, the same sound, creeping under her closed door, spreading into the dark corner by the dresser, and out again, rippling across the floor.

Oh, God, please, she thought. *Oh, God, dear God, God, don't let it be what I think it is*.

What she knew it was, because there was not a single doubt what she was hearing, and prayers could not change it: it was her mother's voice. Just as she had heard it the night her mother died.

She knew, too, just when it would stop.

She lay in bed anticipating that awful silence, shivering and listening.

A roar of laughter then, so loud it seemed to rattle the windows; it filled the room and swirled around her until she thought she could feel its physical touch on her bare shoulders, little fingers of it pattering along her spine.

Stop it, stop, stop! she tried to cry, but no sound came from her lips. *Go away, in the name of Heaven, go away.*

It went on, high, piercing, cutting the darkness. She thought surely she could endure no more. She tried again to pray but the prayers would not come, because she knew that if there really were a God, he could never, ever let anyone suffer through this a second time. No God could be that cruel.

The laughter became screams, horrible shrieking sounds, and shouts. What were they doing to her? What had they done? Helen thought she would go stark raving mad herself if it didn't stop.

It did stop. There was that silence, even worse than the screams had been because it came filled with such expectant horror.

Because she knew what would come next.

And it did: the final scream.

Helen screamed with it. She could not help herself; tears streamed down her cheeks, and she threw back her head and screamed her terror.

From somewhere beyond the door, someone called her name. 'Helen?'

Her scream caught in her throat, became a gasping, strangled cry. She looked toward her bedroom door and saw it start to open and, heart pounding, she thought, *Here it comes, at last. I shall meet it face to face, and I will know at last.*

The light spilled in from the hall. Aunt Willa stood in the doorway, feeling for a light switch where there was none.

'Helen, what's wrong, are you all right?'

'Aunt Willa,' she cried. She bounded out of bed and across the room, to fling her arms about her aunt, so glad to see even her, to see anyone real and human and warm.

'Oh, God, it was horrible,' she said, clinging to her aunt. 'You know who it was, don't you? It was my mother. That was how she died that night, laughing and screaming, just like that.'

'Helen, you're hysterical. Where the hell is the light switch?'

'There, on the dresser.' Helen pointed, laughing with relief.

Aunt Willa found the light, turned it on. Its brightness sent the shadows scurrying back into the corners.

Helen swallowed her laughter and looked around at her familiar room, but it looked entirely unfamiliar, the colors too bright, the edges too sharp.

'What on earth happened to you?' Aunt Willa demanded. 'You scared me half out of my wits, screaming the way you did.'

Helen laughed again, nervously this time, and wrapped her arms about herself. 'That wasn't me,' she said, almost giddy now with relief. She would never have imagined that she should be so glad to see her aunt, so grateful for her company, but she was. 'Just at the end. I mean, that *was* me; but the rest of it, the laughing and the screaming, that wasn't me, it was Mother. That's exactly how she screamed . . . '

She caught her breath abruptly and fell silent. Something in Aunt Willa's face suddenly sobered her.

'What are you babbling about? What screaming and laughing?'

'Didn't you hear . . . ?' She stopped again. She had a terrible sinking sensation, as if she were falling, tumbling down into an impenetrable darkness, where something evil waited.

Her aunt seemed to recede, to move further and further away from her until there was a vast gulf between them, and when Aunt Willa spoke her voice came from a distant universe an eternity away.

She hadn't heard. Helen knew that even before her aunt spoke. This was just another delusion.

Oh God, help me, I'm losing my mind. Help me, someone, please.

'I heard you scream, that's all,' Aunt Willa said. 'I thought . . . you must have been having a nightmare. Jesus, you scared me half to death.'

★　★　★

'Are you sure you want to stay here alone?' Aunt Willa asked. They had come into the hall. Her suede car coat was flung about her shoulders and she carried her overnight bag.

'I'm not alone. Mrs. Hauptman is here.'

'Yes, of course she is, but not at night. And, last night . . . '

'I had a bad dream. That's all it was. Everyone has them occasionally. I'm sure you must have had one at one time or another. There's no reason to dwell on it.'

'Well, if you had seen yourself, how awful you looked . . . And to be honest, you don't look so great this morning. You're as white as a sheet.'

'I'm fine,' Helen said, a bit sharply. She was still half-afraid Aunt Willa might yet change her mind and stay on; and whatever else she might have to endure in the next few days, Helen was sure she could not endure that as well.

The truth was, she had been surprised, mystified even, to discover that Aunt Willa still meant to leave this morning. She had a notion that her aunt had scored a triumph of some sort or other. Certainly her hysteria of the night before must have played right into Aunt Willa's hands, given her the ammunition she needed in any legal manipulations.

It occurred to her, though, that her aunt had been badly frightened herself. For the moment, anyway, she was glad to be leaving the house. Later, perhaps, she would see things differently, but for now what she most wanted was to get away.

'I don't see why Robbie can't come and stay with you for a while. Did you ask her? I'm sure she'd be willing, if you asked.'

'No. I didn't ask. I want to be by myself for a while. I want everybody to see that I am perfectly all right. I don't need to be taken care of like a helpless child.'

Aunt Willa got into the big gray Mercedes and started the motor. She put the window down and scrutinized her niece, looking her up and down.

'But are you all right, is the question. You scared the bejesus out of me last night, I don't mind telling you, screaming like a banshee. If you ask me, I think if you can't get someone to stay here with you, then maybe you should go somewhere else. Somewhere you'll have people to look after you.'

'I don't need anyone to look after me,' Helen said firmly. Now that Aunt Willa was actually in her car, with the motor running, and obviously getting ready to leave, she felt more confident. 'I can look after myself. And there is nothing crazy about that.'

Aunt Willa lifted one perfectly shaped eyebrow slightly. 'Well, I didn't say you were crazy. I'm sure I didn't use that word.'

Helen stepped back from the car. 'Goodbye,' she said. 'It was kind of you to come and see how I'm doing.'

Aunt Willa hesitated for a second or two, about to say something more, and then thought better of it. 'Goodbye,' she said. 'I'll stop back again in a little while and see how you're doing.'

'You should call before you come,' Helen said. 'I may be away or something.'

Aunt Willa had been looking down at the car's dashboard but now her head snapped around. 'Are you planning to go somewhere?' she asked.

Helen, who had only made the remark to discourage another unexpected visit, felt amused; and she said mischievously, giving a shrug, 'I don't know. I may do some traveling. I have all that money now, I suppose I may as well use it.'

Robbie had told her that Aunt Willa had been decrying a shortage of money lately that had stood in the way of a trip she had wanted to take to the Riviera. Her lips tightened a little, but she managed to say in a civil voice, 'You may as well,' and without further comment she drove off down the driveway.

Inside, Mrs. Hauptman was dusting. Helen had the impression the house-keeper was watching her out of the corner of her eye. No doubt she had heard of last night's 'bad dreams.' Perhaps the house-keeper had been recruited to keep an eye on her and report to Aunt Willa.

Helen went through the house and out onto the terrace. Her nerves were stretched taut. Before her the hours of the day were a torturous path that led to another night, and God alone knew what fresh terrors.

She had no idea what she should do. Several times she made up her mind that she must follow everyone's advice and leave the house. She was unaccustomed to taking action, however, and as quickly as she reached this peak, she slid back into the valley of indecision.

She put off doing anything. Twice she went back into the house, meaning to call Robbie and ask her to come down. The second time, she brought Robbie's phone number up on her cellphone before she turned the phone off.

Robbie would think she was crazy. No amount of affection or responsibility would prevent Robbie from reaching that conclusion. Robbie was the only person in the world who could be said to be on her side. She could not bring herself to risk that loyalty. Not just yet.

In the end, Helen decided to do nothing until she saw what happened this coming night. What if Aunt Willa had been right and it had only been a bad dream? However real it seemed to her, it might have been a dream, might it not? Some dreams did seem that real.

She would wait one more night, and of one thing she was certain: Tonight she would not dream. If anything should happen, she would know.

Then, if she must, she would call Robbie.

★　★　★

Nothing happened. Nothing.

She took one of the tranquilizers that Doctor Martin had given her before she left the clinic, and deliberated over a sleeping pill before deciding against it. She wanted to stay awake. It was the only way she could really know. If it had somehow been just a dream, it could not trouble her if she were awake. And if it were not a dream, then she was better off staying awake to cope with it.

She sat and read in the chair in her room, turning the chair so that it directly faced the door. She had locked the door with a big old key she had found in the kitchen. She considered placing the dresser against the door as well. She did not know if whatever she had heard in the house could get through locked doors. If it could, then it could no doubt get through dressers as well.

At first she read for no more than a minute or two at a time, only to find herself watching the door expectantly, anxiously. But as the hours crept by and nothing happened, she became less concerned.

Sometime late in the night she fell asleep. It was morning when she woke, to discover that nothing had happened. She felt nearly giddy with relief.

Nothing happened the next night either, or the night after, or the night after that. It became apparent that however real the disturbances had seemed to her, they had indeed been only part of her dreams.

Her life did not suddenly become one of unbridled happiness as a result of this conclusion. Some of the tension disappeared, it was true, and she slept better, with no recurrence of the dreams.

She still lived in her isolation, however,

conscious of her separation from others. She still sometimes imagined the old fantasies, of being like other people, having friends, perhaps experiencing romance. She thought of Robbie's friend, whom she had never met. Was there someone like that out there somewhere for her? She tried to imagine what it would be like, to be with someone in that way, but she had no experience upon which to build those fantasies.

But she had no hope that any of this would really come true either.

Sometimes she went out, a time or two to the cemetery, and again to shop in the local stores. She did this more than anything else to try to accomplish some touch of oneness with the outside world, with other people. Once she stopped to look at the posters in the window of a travel agency. She thought of traveling. But that filled her with dread too. How could she cope with all the problems that travel surely entailed?

She had talked briefly to Robbie of her old wish to be free, but she was no freer now than she had ever been. The past, her old habits, fear, the very makeup of her personality, all conspired to imprison her and cut her off from the world as surely as if she had been invisible. Indeed, she began to think of herself that way.

Robbie called several times during the next month. It was plain that her sister did not like telephones. She gave the impression of regretting what she regarded as her duty. Each time she called, she suggested that she could come for a visit if Helen needed her.

'It's not like I'm at the end of my rope,' Helen told her. Robbie's discomfort on the phone made her uncomfortable too.

'Well, I can be there in practically no time if you need me. All you have to do is say the word.'

'Things are all right now. They were a little strange at first, but it's better now.'

'In what way strange?' Robbie sounded worried.

'Oh, look, don't you start psychoanalyzing me. I promise when we get together I'll tell you all about it. Just now you'd think I'm crazy.'

Robbie laughed and said, 'I guess as

long as you can make remarks like that, you aren't. But you will call if . . . well, if anything? Promise?'

Aunt Willa did not call. Helen supposed Mrs. Hauptman kept her up to date. Truth to tell, Mrs. Hauptman's reports must be very disappointing — unless she embellished them a bit, which seemed unlike Mrs. Hauptman, who she thought singularly lacking in imagination.

Nothing happened. Not for a full month.

★   ★   ★

This time it was her father. Helen sat shivering in her bed and listened to the ruckus outside her door. She heard all the yelling and the shouting and the crashing of furniture and even the gunshots.

Because she had been through it all before, she could follow in great detail the progress of the struggle, from its inception right through to its grim conclusion at the foot of the stairs.

She was sick with fright. She could tell, though, when the episode was over, because the awful cold that had come into her room and awakened her lessened, until the room grew warm again.

The two men did not come into her room, however. She was spared that reenactment, but her relief was mingled with some other strange emotion that she could not put a name to.

She had learned one thing, though. It happened with the full moon, just as on that first night, the night of the actual events, when there had been a full moon.

So she had a month in which to get help.

Part II

Robbie

12

'So why does she have to come here?' Joe asked. 'If she's got all that damned money, why can't she go stay at a hotel someplace?'

He was a big man, bulging with muscles, and with a slight beer belly that distorted the line of his tee shirt. Despite several years of college, which he had spent playing football, he was not very intelligent.

'It wasn't his mind that appealed to me,' Robbie was fond of explaining to their friends. 'He just has all the right instincts.'

'Because,' she said now, addressing Joe as one would a stubborn child, 'she is my sister and she is coming to visit me for the first time ever. Look, Joe, it won't hurt you in the slightest. And I'm paying for your room, right?'

'Wrong. *This* is my room,' he said, with an emphatic sweep of one beefy hand. 'Why can't I stay here anyway? What the hell, doesn't she know about boys and girls?'

Robbie smiled a little wryly. 'Frankly, I don't think so. Take my word for it, we would all be uncomfortable. Now be reasonable, honey. And do hurry, she'll be here any minute.'

'It's damn short notice,' Joe grumbled, shoving some boxer shorts into a canvas flight bag that was his sole piece of luggage.

'It's short notice for me, too,' Robbie said. She had not even known Helen was coming until she was virtually here, calling from Grand Central to say she had decided upon a visit. And something about Helen's voice, about the nonchalance and the unnatural brightness of it, had told her that Helen needed her in some way. So, like it or not, Joe had to go. If something was bothering Helen, Joe's presence would certainly inhibit her from talking about it.

Still grumbling, Joe allowed himself to be shepherded out the door, on his way to a small rented hotel room a block away.

'When will I see you?' he asked, pausing in the door.

'When I can,' Robbie snapped; and then, seeing the hurt expression in Joe's quite childlike eyes, she stretched on tiptoe to kiss him. 'Silly, do you think I won't miss you too? I'll get together with you somehow.'

Helen arrived minutes later, looking flushed with the excitement of making her own way in a taxi from the station. Robbie saw that she was very keyed up, more than from just the trip, but she let it go for a while and kept up a flow of welcoming chatter while Helen settled in, taking off her coat and gloves, making a trip to the tiny bathroom.

' . . . such a wonderful surprise,' Robbie said from the other room. 'I'd have been happy to have you up sooner, but you sounded so determined about staying in that gloomy old house. What changed your mind anyway?'

Helen came back into the combination living-room-bedroom. 'Nothing in particular. I just thought maybe a few days in the city would . . . I don't know. Would something.'

'And they will, too,' Robbie said,

putting an arm about her sister's shoulders. 'Do you know, this is the first time you've ever come to visit me in all these years?'

'I couldn't before.'

'I know, he'd never have permitted it. Are you hungry? How about we go get some lunch?'

'Fine.' Helen paused and then said, 'Robbie, about your friend — I could stay at a hotel, you know. I didn't mean to put him out. To tell you the truth, I completely forgot about him.'

'My what?' Robbie looked blank for a moment, then laughed and gave a gesture of dismissal. 'Honey, you're so cute when you try to skirt issues. He's not my friend, he's my lover. Anyway, he moved out ages ago. He didn't just leave so there would be room for you. Now, don't you worry about him. What in heaven's name made you think of him, anyway?'

'When he 'moved out ages ago', he forgot to take his shaving things out of the bathroom cabinet,' Helen said with a smile. 'The razor's still warm.'

Robbie looked surprised. She went into

the bathroom and saw for herself that Joe had left behind his electric razor, his colognes, everything of his that had been there. Probably left it on purpose, she thought. When she came back out, she had a mock-guilty look.

'Well, maybe he's growing a beard,' she said with a shrug. She laughed and hugged Helen. 'Let's go out and eat something. You'll suffer through my cooking soon enough. And believe me, it will make you look upon Hauptman in a new light of affection.'

'I don't think anything could accomplish that,' Helen said, wrinkling her nose.

They had lunch in a shiny little place that advertised 'Hidden Health.' Helen didn't quite recognize any of the dishes Robbie ordered for her, but at Robbie's prodding she nodded and agreed they were very good. The restaurant was owned by a friend of Robbie's, a male friend named Bill. All of Robbie's friends were male, it began to appear.

'And who's this?' Bill demanded. 'Have you brought me a present for my birthday?'

'Your birthday's not until next June,' Robbie said. 'And my sister is already spoken for, thank you very much.'

'Spoken for?' Helen said when he had gone.

'Oh, Bill is impossible. If he thought you were available, he'd be sitting in your lap before we got our lunch.'

Watching her sister as they ate, Helen envied Robbie her easy confidence and the natural flow of conversation, even with strangers. Robbie was as casual and breezy with someone who had just come in off the street as she had always been with Helen herself.

Helen could not talk freely, not even with Robbie. She had come up to the city on an impulse, telephoning Robbie from the station with the excuse that she had an urge to see New York City. The truth was that she had no one else in the world, other than Robbie, to whom she could turn.

The house was haunted. Or, alternatively, she was out of her mind. But she did not like to consider that alternative. She was convinced that she had seen what she had seen and heard what she had heard. Something was manifesting itself in that house, something that was supernatural.

She had never asked herself before whether she believed in the supernatural, in ghosts and the like. Never before had there been any need even to consider the matter.

Now there was clearly a need. She could not but believe. She had heard the voices of her parents: her mother laughing and sobbing hysterically as she died whatever gruesome death she had suffered; her father, shouting and swearing as he was killed fighting off his attackers. She had heard these voices, replaying as it were their parts in that grim drama long after the actual events had occurred.

Her parents were in their graves, but something, some part of them, lingered in the house, haunting her. This was real, or she could no longer trust her mind at all.

How could she tell Robbie these things, though? She sipped something that Robbie described vaguely as a 'protein drink,' and looked across the little metal table at her sister. Robbie, with her bright eyes and her bleached hair. Robbie was alive, utterly alive. What traffic could she have with the dead?

Robbie, who had watched these various thoughts chase one another across Helen's face, suddenly put her cup down with a bang and said, 'You're going to have to tell me sometime.'

Helen started and said, 'What?'

'Something is bugging you. You've been sitting there for fifteen minutes not listening to a single thing I've said, and stewing over something. Now, tell big sister what it is.'

'I might just have come to see you and the city,' Helen said, putting explanation off. She glanced down at the muddy liquid in her cup. It looked as bad as it tasted.

'Oh, sure,' Robbie said dryly. When Helen did not reply at once, she said tentatively, 'It's Aunt Willa, isn't it?'

Helen's eyes went wide. 'Aunt Willa?'

'She came to see you. And she bugged you.' Robbie had the air of someone who was satisfied she had learned what she wanted to know. She had put this explanation together in her mind the last few minutes, watching Helen. Helen was the sort to let Aunt Willa get under her skin.

'Look honey, she called me. I know all about everything you did while she was there, including the fact that you had a bad dream. For Christ's sake, Joe usually has to punch me once a week to wake me up from some creepy-crawly I'm dreaming up. It's nothing to get into a blue funk over.'

Tell her, tell her, a voice shrilled inside Helen's head.

'Am I right?'

'I guess you're right,' Helen said in a resigned voice. The moment of opportunity slid by.

'I knew it. Listen, all you need is a chance to relax a little. I'm so glad you've come up to town. We're going to have a ball, the two of us, and you won't ever want to go back to that gloomy old barn. And if you have a bad dream while you're sleeping with me, I shall simply kick you in the butt and tell you to be quiet.'

Partly because of the tension she had

been under, and partly because she knew Robbie would do just what she threatened, Helen began incongruously to giggle. The giggle became rapidly an honest-to-goodness laughing fit, in which Robbie was only too happy to join. This was what she had wanted: to get Helen laughing, to make her forget Aunt Willa and that gloomy house and bad dreams.

The two of them sat leaning across the table, laughing, Helen trying to smother her laughter because she could see people were looking at them. Robbie didn't care at all if anybody looked. Helen's face was streaked with tears by the time she finally got herself under control, but when Robbie said, her voice sliding off into another howl, 'And I'm going to wear my hiking boots to bed,' they were off again.

This is ridiculous, Helen told herself, but she laughed on until she had exhausted the last of her meager store of merriment. Across from her, watching despite her laughter, Robbie thought, *Isn't this wonderful? This was all Helen needed.*

When they were more or less themselves again, Robbie said, 'Come on, let's do some sightseeing. When were you last in town?'

'I came in with Father the last time about ten years ago,' Helen said.

'And with him, I'm sure you didn't get to have any fun. We'll make up for that, though, I promise you. It's going to be nothing but fun, your whole visit. I forbid a single serious thought.'

And so, Helen told herself, I cannot tell her about it, not now anyway. Not after that command, and when she's trying so hard to cheer me up. I'll tell her later, when it won't seem so serious. One night when we're in bed and we can laugh about it, and she will tell me how silly I was to be so frightened.

Anyway, it really wasn't something she wanted to talk about. She was glad of an excuse to put it off. And until she got ready to return home, until the next full moon, it wasn't all that critical. That was when she needed to worry about it, and by then they would be at ease with one another.

She thought fleetingly, *Robbie is already at ease — but I may never be.*

13

And they did do a lot in the next few days. Robbie's chief medicine for any problem was keeping busy, and she set herself to keeping Helen busy as well, seeing the city.

It seemed to Helen as if they must have seen everything that was even remotely worthwhile in the place, plus a few things that were not. Everything was seen in short, rapid little bursts of exploration because that was the way Robbie did things.

Helen was certain they had ridden every subway. They pushed and raced through Times Square — 'We won't want to spend any time here' — and were shot, as if from a cannon, in a high-speed elevator to the top of the Empire State Building. Robbie, who had been here before and was getting a little tired of sightseeing, took a quick peek over the railing before whisking them down again.

They saw Radio City Music Hall, but not for a movie, just long enough to catch part of the show.

Only the ride on the ferry to the Statue of Liberty moved at a reasonable pace, and Helen thought from the way Robbie kept peering down at the dark-looking water that she would have preferred to get out and swim, to get there faster.

'There's so much to see and do here,' Robbie said, trying to revitalize enthusiasm. 'Isn't it exciting?'

'It's certainly . . . ' Helen paused to consider just what she thought the city was. ' . . . busy,' she concluded lamely.

It was entirely different from what she remembered from visits with her father. Of course, those visits had been conducted at a very leisurely pace. Not even the frenzy of life in Manhattan could have daunted her father, or altered his lifestyle.

And she, Helen, had seen everything from within a solidly insulated glass cage: seeing out, seeing everything — or as much as Father gave her permission to see — but not touching anything; and never, never being touched. Like when people ran into her now, on the sidewalk. She had stopped complaining about it to Robbie, who only said, 'It's a big city,' or, 'Everything is so full here, even the sidewalks.'

To Helen the city was a jumbled impression, blasting loud and brilliantly lighted, and all rushing swiftly past and about her, always going in exactly the opposite direction from the one in which she was traveling. At least it did seem to her that no one, nothing, was ever traveling in the same direction as she was, although of course that was only her imagination. And if she tried to stop, tried to stand still for a moment to get her bearings, all that motion and activity whirled and eddied about her, like water in a river rapids surging about a rock until it had dislodged it and could move it along as well.

'I never thought to ask,' Robbie said, turning from the dark water to look expectantly at her. 'Is there anything in particular you want to do?'

'Sit down somewhere and prop my feet up,' Helen said, a bit ruefully.

Robbie laughed and said, 'You are so funny. I think it's done you a world of good being here.' She had been thinking all day how much better Helen looked. On the other hand, she herself had problems: Joe, for one.

They were in a taxi, rushing through Central Park on their way to a cocktail party. It was Sunday afternoon and Helen felt as if she had not had a chance to rest since she had arrived.

'Never mind about the neighborhood,' Robbie said, leaning toward the window to look out at the houses going by. 'Lisa has been looking for months and she was lucky to get this. Apartments are scarce and cost a fortune. You wouldn't believe how long I looked for that dump I'm in.'

Helen knew it was only her imagination in thinking that phrase, 'cost a fortune,' was emphasized. Robbie would never emphasize that. Robbie knew, after all, that she could have however much she wanted of her sister's money. Helen had told her that, right from the beginning.

'Robbie, you know, if you ever need anything . . . ' she started to say yet again, but Robbie interrupted her, tapping on the glass that separated them from the driver.

'This is it,' she said.

Inside Lisa's apartment, the walls were lined with bookcases made of bricks and unpainted boards. The furniture was mostly studio beds piled high with assorted pillows in a riot of colors, and tables that were really old trunks — one of them a wooden packing crate that had been used to ship liquor.

'It's charming,' Helen said when Robbie prompted her with, 'Don't you love Lisa's apartment?'

Although there were only a few people when they got there, the room quickly got very noisy and very full. The air was close and the conversations had become all muddled and fragmented, so that Helen, trying to follow them all, could hardly keep clear in her mind who was speaking to whom, or about what.

Robbie drifted away and came back with a young man in tow. She introduced him to Helen, and was gone again. This time, she seemed to have just disappeared.

'I don't understand why you didn't stay at the party until I got back,' Robbie complained. 'I fixed you up with Larry. He's hot.'

Robbie refilled her coffee cup and banged the pot back on the stove so hard that it rattled. She had with considerable difficulty managed to restrain her own temper and get a frustrated Joe quickly out of the apartment.

'I didn't like Larry.' Helen put her hands to her burning cheeks and pressed, squeezing her mouth all out of shape.

'There are women, plenty of them, who would kill for a chance at Larry.'

'I was scared. In a strange place, with all those strange people. Once I realized you'd gone, I didn't want to stay there, with or without Larry. I came straight here. I thought . . . I don't even know what I thought. I must have thought something.'

Robbie sighed and some of the rigidity went out of her shoulders. She ought to have known how uncomfortable Helen would be. She had never had a chance to get used to parties and people and lots of commotion.

'You could at least have rung the bell when you got here,' she said, more gently.

'I didn't think.' Helen pushed the flesh up over her cheekbones, crushing her eyes into narrow slits. She was trying hard not to think about the scene she had walked in on: Robbie and Joe, doing something. She was not entirely sure what it was called, but there was no mistaking its purpose.

They sat in silence for a long moment. 'I guess now you'll be going home,' Robbie said finally.

'I'm afraid to go home,' Helen said.

'Why? I mean, all that stuff that happened, sure, but that was a long time ago. It can't happen again, you know.'

'It does, though. It happens again. And again and again and again. That whole awful night happens again every month.'

'What are you talking about? You mean those nightmares of yours?'

'I mean the house is haunted.'

Robbie's eyes went wide and she set

her cup absentmindedly aside. 'Do you mean you've seen ghosts?' she asked, watching her sister closely.

Helen took her hands away from her face and it fell into its familiar shape. She looked drawn and tired and there were lines about her eyes caused by the fear that had been nagging at her constantly.

'Not seen,' she said. 'Heard. I hear them. Father, the others, all of them. I hear everything, just the way it happened that night.'

Robbie let her remarks sink in. It was incredible to think that such a thing could happen, to Helen of all people. She herself had no particular belief or disbelief in ghosts. She believed in other sorts of psychic phenomena, didn't she? She had a girlfriend who was wonderful with horoscopes, and another who insisted she was a witch. And she'd had experiences of her own that she had considered psychic at the time.

But, ghosts? And with Helen — who, one had to face it, had had some troubles the last few years.

She slowly pulled out a chair, never

taking her eyes from Helen's face, and sat at the table opposite her.

'Tell me everything about it,' she said.

★ ★ ★

It was several days before they could drive down to the house. Robbie went about her preparations as if she were planning an around-the-world cruise.

'But there's everything you need at the house already,' Helen pointed out.

'Maybe there's everything *you* need in that tomb,' Robbie said, 'but I am used to a different lifestyle.'

So it was necessary to go shopping, which Robbie did with a vengeance. Helen tried to pay for her purchases, but Robbie wouldn't permit that either.

There was a quarrel with Joe, who could not understand why it was suddenly so important that Robbie accompany her sister home. Robbie had promised Helen not to tell anyone the real reason, not until she herself had seen what was really going on.

'If she doesn't want to stay here,' Joe

argued, 'why can't she just go home alone? Why do you have to go?'

'Because she's been sick,' Robbie said, 'and I don't think she should be alone just now.'

'Then hire her a babysitter, for crap's sake.'

'Now, sweetie,' Robbie said, and set herself to coaxing Joe out of his bad humor. She succeeded, but just barely, and only after promising she would stay no more than a week — which was all the time she could take off work anyway.

The day before they were to leave, Robbie went out alone on a mysterious errand, the nature of which she refused to disclose to Helen.

'You'll find out soon enough,' was all she would say.

She was back in a short while, holding something under her coat.

'*Et voila*,' she said, opening her coat to reveal a small brown-and-white puppy.

'A dog? But what on earth . . . ?'

'His name is Tiger and he's going with us.' Robbie put the dog down and he immediately began to explore his new surroundings, working his way cautiously closer to where Helen was standing. Tiger was little more than a mutt, with large friendly eyes and an active tail.

Helen was doubtful. 'I don't know,' she said hesitantly. 'You know how Father always felt about pets in the house. And Mrs. Hauptman . . . '

'Father isn't there. Not in the flesh, anyway. And Hauptman will fuss, but that's nothing unusual; she fusses all the time anyway.' She did a comical imitation of Mrs. Hauptman's scowling expression and her irritated voice. ' 'I can't come full-time and I won't work at night.' '

Helen laughed. 'I guess you're right.'

'I know I am. We need a dog. They're much more sensitive to spirits and things. If there's anything there at all, he'll sense it long before we do. We'll have advance notice, so to speak.'

Although Helen wasn't sure they needed advance notice.

14

At first, it really was kind of fun. Robbie's spirits were so buoyant, so infectious, that Helen found herself actually feeling giddy and adventurous at being back in the house.

'We won't tell Hauptman anything about the visitations,' Robbie dictated as they were driving down. 'She was nervous enough about coming back. If she knew we even suspected there were ghosts in the house, she would set a new track record getting out of there.'

Robbie made a joke of everything that had happened before, and because it was a secret from Mrs. Hauptman, or from anyone else for that matter, it became a source of great giggling and gesturing. Behind Mrs. Hauptman's back, Robbie would point silently at the banister and wring her hands, Lady-Macbeth-style, as if she were wringing blood from them.

And Helen, who had been scared out of

her wits by just that occurrence with the blood on the stairs, found herself laughing about it and wondering how she had ever been so frightened. The terror that the house had inspired in her now seemed unreal, and she began to wonder if perhaps after all she had just imagined everything.

'We'll soon know,' Robbie said. 'Anyway, you've got plenty of reason to be afraid, because if nothing happens on the night of the full moon, I am going to be ribbing you about this for the rest of your life, trust me.'

'Fine,' Helen said. 'In that case I'll cover myself with a sheet and hover beside your bed during the night.'

'You'd better make sure to hover out of kicking range. I always go down fighting.'

Despite his friendly overtures in her direction, Tiger met with Mrs. Hauptman's expected disapproval. 'I can't be responsible for what you find in your soup,' she said ominously.

'Within reasonable limits,' Robbie corrected her.

Mrs. Hauptman left the room in a huff, and Robbie gave Tiger an extravagant hug.

The dog gave no sign of sensing any foreign presence in the house. He quickly made himself at home, sharing the bedroom with the sisters at night and staying close to one or the other of them during the day. He seemed altogether pleased with his new quarters.

It snowed as the month neared its end, the first snow of the season. Helen and Robbie went out to play in the new-fallen snow like a pair of children.

'Only,' Robbie said, 'we never got to do anything like this when we were children.'

They made a snowman and threw snowballs at one another, and romped with Tiger, and all three of them earned Mrs. Hauptman's further disapproval by tracking snow into her clean kitchen.

The house, for all its poor lighting and antiquated design, actually seemed to absorb Robbie's high spirits, and for the first time ever it seemed to Helen a happy place, a charming old house that glowed and warmed. Fires burned in the fireplaces and in the evenings, after Mrs. Hauptman had gone, they roasted hot dogs and marshmallows, drank chocolate or munched popcorn, while the dog dozed on the hearth and begged an occasional scrap of food.

Mostly, they talked. They talked of everything and nothing, and they avoided only one subject: their relationship with their father. As if by mutual consent, he never entered into their conversation.

Later, Helen would remember that brief time of Robbie's visit. It would stand out like an oasis in a desert, a brief breathing space. It was almost too beautiful. Despite the chill of winter and the snow that lingered on the ground, the days were sunny, the skies cloudless and a luminous silvery blue.

Then Helen began to think ahead. By the time another full moon came around after this one, it would be Christmas. She thought of putting up a tree. Maybe Robbie would come down again — this time with Joe, of course. They'd have a real Christmas feast: roast goose, maybe. She'd never actually had that before.

They'd never really had Christmas before, in fact; their father thought it was a waste of time and money.

Though she did not say so, Robbie had concluded by this time that the 'ghosts' were nothing more than Helen's over-worked imagination and the strain she had been under. Nothing out of the ordinary had happened since they had arrived. The dog was blissfully unaware of any hauntings. And Helen herself acted as if she had forgotten them.

'I shouldn't have left her alone down here, not at first,' Robbie told herself, and vowed that she would be more consider-ate in the future.

The days passed by, liquid, hurrying down to the end of the month. And, suddenly, as if a switch had been thrown, Helen woke one morning to find the world outside her window was gray and dreary. Tonight was the full moon, and the sky, the whole world, seemed to have just now remembered it. The house, only the day before gay and cheerful, was once again dark and gloomy, and from the shadows in the corners morbid fancies taunted her.

'Hey, come on,' Robbie said over breakfast. 'No long faces, okay? Nothing has changed since yesterday, you know.'

'But it has. Everything's changed. Can't you feel it, the tension in the air?'

'No, all I feel is your dismal mood. That's the only thing that's changed. If you were like this before, it's no wonder you heard things.'

But for Helen, everything had changed. Even Robbie was different. Her laugh suddenly seemed to ring hollow, and as the day wore on, even Robbie stopped pretending that things were the same.

'It's your fault, damn it,' Robbie said as evening began to darken the rooms. 'You've been going around all day looking over your shoulder and jumping every time a board creaks. You've got me doing it. It's contagious. You have got to stop it.'

Robbie was annoyed with herself, too, for feeling jittery. She blamed Helen for making her nervous. Of course the place had the atmosphere of a haunted house. Helen herself was haunting it with her fear.

'Don't you feel it?' Helen asked, instinctively lowering her voice as if someone might be listening, although

Mrs. Hauptman had already gone for the day and they were alone in the house except for Tiger.

'There's a feeling of something here,' Helen insisted. 'As if you could turn and see it, almost. Like someone whispering in the next room, whispers you can't quite hear and yet you nearly can.'

'I don't hear or feel anything,' Robbie said, a shrill note of anger creeping into her voice. This was really getting to be a drag. 'Except the tension you're creating by being so wound up. For God's sake, won't you just relax and stop harping on what you imagine you feel?'

Helen did stop talking about it then, but she could still feel it, and she was sure it was not just something she was imagining. Something was here with them now, something as real as those screams she had heard, as real as the sounds of struggle outside her bedroom door. Something — she didn't know what to call it; a presence, she guessed — that hadn't been here during the preceding days but was present now.

She could feel it in the rooms with

them. She could almost hear what it thought. It knew that Robbie was here. It knew that Robbie was frightened too and did not want to admit it, because she had not yet seen or heard anything. Robbie was so practical.

But practicality was not enough for some situations. Practicality would not spare them from what was in store for them. Helen did not know what it was, but she was sure, as sure as she had ever been of anything, that the night before them would be like nothing she had ever experienced before.

★   ★   ★

She had been sure that she would not sleep at all, but Helen did fall asleep with surprisingly little difficulty, grateful at least for the presence of Robbie in the bed next to hers.

When she woke, it was gradually, and at first without knowing why. For a few seconds she lay in bed, listening to the silence, wondering what had awakened her.

Then, slowly, she became aware of the cold: intense, burning cold. She wrapped the covers snugly about herself and still she was shivering. Each second seemed to increase the chill.

She listened, and knew Robbie was awake too, and wondered what she was thinking now.

'Robbie, oh God, you must be able to feel that,' Helen whispered into the darkness.

'I don't feel anything,' Robbie said after a pause, but she sounded unconvincing. Her voice in the dark was tremulous, and Helen knew that it was not only from the icy chill that had completely invaded the room.

'The cold. Oh, Robbie, I'm freezing. I think I'm going to be sick.'

It was colder than it had ever been before, terribly, terribly cold, and Helen was more frightened than she had been before. She had a sudden knowledge that this was different somehow from everything up to now. This time it would be worse, far worse.

Robbie got up quickly from her bed and came to Helen's, slipping under the covers with her and hugging her tightly.

'It's all right, really,' she said, 'don't be scared.'

'But don't you feel it, can't you feel the cold?' Helen clung to her, trying to absorb some warmth from Robbie's body.

Robbie sighed. 'Yes, I feel it, of course I do. The furnace has gone out, that's all. You're forgetting it's winter outside. In a minute I'll go downstairs and see if I can get it started again.'

She did not go, however, because in the next moment the noises had begun.

Helen did not say *I told you so*. She clung desperately to her sister as if she were sinking and Robbie was her only hope of salvation.

She knew every sound, every crash and bang, every cry of pain and horror, every whoosh of knife cutting air. She tried not to listen and wished something would stop the cold. She felt no warmth, even with Robbie's arms around her. She might have been dead already, in the cold of the tomb, beyond the warmth of life. Icy shivers ran across her shoulders and along her spine.

Someone screamed aloud, 'For God's

sake, stop it! Please!'

With a shock, Helen realized it was she who had shouted.

The noise did stop. The house suddenly sat about them in utter silence. Not a board creaked. Not even a leaf rustled in the tree beyond the window.

'I think it's over,' Robbie said in a cracking whisper.

Helen shook her head violently and her body trembled convulsively. Never, not in her worst nightmares, had she dreamed it was possible to feel so horrified.

'It's not over,' she said through clattering teeth. 'They are out there. They are listening. Robbie, what are we going to do?'

'For one thing,' Robbie said, taking a deep breath, 'we are going to turn on a light.' She started to get up from the bed but Helen held on to her frantically.

'Don't leave me, oh my God, Robbie, don't leave me,' she sobbed.

'Okay, then come with me, baby, I'm only going to the dresser.' Robbie was trying to sound brave, but even her voice was quavering, and Helen could feel her shivering too.

They got out of bed together, a clumsy process because Helen would not relinquish her hold on Robbie's neck. Stumbling together, they managed to cross the room to the dresser. The light switch clicked under Robbie's fingers, and the light splashed into the room.

'Robbie, look. Tiger.'

Helen had completely forgotten that poor animal, but as the light came on they saw him. The dog seemed to have been asleep but now he sat up, his ears twitching, his nose sniffing. He fixed his eyes on Helen, and his stare was so strange that Helen found her attention riveted upon the little animal. Slowly Tiger rose to his feet, bristling, his stare even wilder, and he stood rigidly.

'The poor creature is scared out of his senses,' Robbie said, reaching out a hand toward him.

'Don't touch him,' Helen said. In the same moment, an arctic wind blew through the room, as if a door or a window had suddenly been flung open. They both whirled about, expecting to see the bedroom door standing open. It was still firmly closed.

It seemed to Helen though as if the door was far, far away, a mile or more from where they were standing. It almost looked, and felt, as if the air between them and the door was in motion, churning.

We are lost, Helen thought. *They are here with us, and it is over for me, I can no longer resist him. He can possess me, if that's what he wants. It's what he always wanted, what he always did, and I can no longer fight that.*

'Don't say that,' Robbie said. Helen did not realize she had spoken aloud — did not know, in fact, what she had said — and she looked stupidly at her sister.

'Let me put you back to bed,' Robbie said in a gentler tone. 'I think it's over now.'

'But you heard it, didn't you? You did hear it, Robbie, say you did . . . oh!' She looked back at Tiger, to discover that the dog had slunk into a corner of the wall as if to press his way through it. He was beside himself with fright, baring his teeth, his eyes huge in his tiny head.

15

Suddenly, the cold was gone. There was no rush of warm air. Simply, it had been cold and now it was warm.

'This time it really is over,' Robbie said, and no sooner had the words come from her mouth than the laughing began. 'Lord,' she whispered, 'who . . . ?'

She suddenly realized who and jerked her head around to stare open-mouthed at Helen. 'No. It can't be.'

'Where are you going?' Helen cried. Robbie had suddenly started across the room toward the door.

'It's Mother, isn't it? It's coming from her room. I'm going to go see. I'm not going to spend the rest of the night cowering in here like a ninny. You can stay here if you want. Lock the door.'

'Don't leave me alone,' Helen begged. 'I'd rather go with you than stay here alone.'

Had the haunters gone? Probably not,

not so long as she and Robbie could hear the laughter, but at least they weren't as vividly here as before.

When Robbie threw open the door to the hall, a fresh gust of cold air hit them, but the hall was empty; and, except for the laughing, that they could hear more clearly now, the house was silent.

Wordlessly, Robbie started along the hall. Helen took only a few seconds to see that the door to their father's room was open, but not for anything would she have gone to that door and looked in. That was more than could be asked of human frailty. Looking from right to left, she followed closely after Robbie.

It was colder in the hall, colder still as they approached the door at the hall's end. The closer they came to their mother's room, the colder Helen felt again.

They reached the door without incident and stopped outside it. The noise was still going on inside. Someone — some *thing* — was laughing, actually roaring with laughter. There was no doubt that it came from within this bedroom. It was awful to hear it, to know that they were separated from the sound only by a thin door.

Then, just as Helen had heard it before, but more distinctly because she was closer than she had ever dared be before, the laughter was cut, cut as if cut with a knife, and she heard a hiss of pain. She hadn't heard that before.

Then they heard a gasp.

And, finally, the shriek. It was a scream that came from the furthest depths of pain and torture. It was followed by groans and gasps. Helen thought she would faint. Her legs felt unable to support her.

All this while, which might have been a minute, perhaps two, she had watched Robbie. Robbie had said nothing since they came into the hall, and so far she had not admitted to actually hearing anything. But Helen knew that she had heard everything too. She had to hear it. And she was obviously frightened, despite her bravado. Her face was ashen, her eyes wide.

Silence.

'It's really stopped now,' Helen said breathless. 'It always ends like that.'

After a pause, Robbie said, 'I'm going

to go in there. I want to see.'

Helen grabbed her arm. 'No, Robbie, no, please, for God's sake. It's over now. That's all there is.'

Robbie turned to look at her. She even smiled, a bit shakily. She was getting her courage back.

'It's all right,' she said. 'You stay out here. I just want to have a look. Is it unlocked?'

Helen blinked. She hadn't even considered that question before. 'I think so. I haven't tried it.'

Robbie put a hand to the knob and turned it. The door opened effortlessly, swinging inward so quickly and easily that someone inside might have opened it for her.

'Robbie,' Helen started to say, but suddenly she felt colder than ever before, deathly cold. She did not want to be alone in the hall and nothing could have persuaded her to go into that room.

'It's all right,' Robbie said again. 'You'll be okay out here. Wait for me.' She went inside.

The door closed after her. Helen could

not say if Robbie had closed it herself or some breeze — there was a draft here — had instead. But a minute later, Robbie said from inside, 'Did you close the door?'

Helen said simply, 'No.'

She waited. The silence went on and on. From within the bedroom she thought she heard footsteps, some hint of movement, muttered words even, but she could not distinguish them.

Abruptly and distinctly, a voice — Robbie's voice, but strangely changed — said, 'Helen, go away.'

Startled by the command, because it was given as a command, Helen said, 'Robbie . . . '

Robbie did not let her finish. 'I want you to go back to your bedroom, right now, go inside and lock your door. Helen, do as I tell you.'

Helen hesitated for a moment, actually taking a step toward the door of her mother's bedroom, thinking, *I ought to go in, I ought to see what's wrong. Robbie may need me.*

As if sensing her indecision, Robbie

said sharply, 'Helen, go, please, do as I say, I beg you.'

Helen went obediently along the hall toward her bedroom, looking over her shoulder at the closed door as she went. When she reached the open door of her own room, however, she stopped and turned back to stare along the hall.

She could not think why Robbie had ordered her away from that door. She was torn between her accustomed obedience to commands and her feeling that she ought to have gone in, to see what, if anything, Robbie had discovered. She cursed herself for a coward and a fool.

At last, when she was on the very verge of retracing her steps down the hallway, the door at its end opened and Robbie came out, closing the door firmly behind herself, and walked quickly along the hall. Helen stepped from her doorway, watching her sister approach.

She was struck by Robbie's appearance. If ever she had seen horror in a human face, it was there. So altered was Robbie that Helen might have met her on a crowded street and not even have recognized her own sister. She looked old, far beyond her years, old and haggard, and in the dim light, utterly dissipated.

Robbie was walking rapidly, almost running, straight down the hall. To Helen's surprise, she looked straight ahead and she did not stop or slow her pace in the slightest when she came to where Helen was standing. She went without pause toward the stairs and only as she passed by Helen did she glance once, fleetingly, in Helen's direction, as if she had never seen her before.

In a whisper that scarcely seemed to come from her lips, she said, 'In the name of all that's holy, leave this place.'

A moment more and she was gone, rushing down the stairs.

Helen was so bewildered she hardly knew what to do. She ran involuntarily to the head of the stairs, forgetting for a moment even to be frightened, and calling, 'Robbie, wait.'

Robbie did not wait. 'Burn it to the ground,' she called back. Clinging to the balusters and taking several steps at a time, she reached the floor below in a matter of seconds. Helen saw her dash across the vestibule, saw her fling open the door and rush out, not even bothering to close it in her wake. The heavy door swung to and fro in the bitter wind that rushed through the house.

Helen was alone.

The house around her seemed to laugh silently.

★　★　★

It was several long seconds before Helen could make herself move. Then she began to run down the steps as Robbie had done.

She had gotten halfway, however, before she stopped, remembering the dog in her bedroom. She could not go, no matter how scared she was, and leave that poor terrified animal to an unknown fate. She ran back up the stairs, trying not to think of what might be in the house with her.

Tiger was still cowering in the corner of the bedroom. As Helen came in, the dog fixed his eyes on her with a look so wild that Helen hesitated to come all the way to where he was and pick him up.

'Come,' she said, but her voice was so shaky that she knew it lacked any authority. The dog made no response. He might not even have heard.

Helen moved toward him, thinking she must try to pick him up and take him out of the house. She knew the terrified animal would never voluntarily come with her into the hall.

But before she could stoop down to pick Tiger up, a sound arrested her: the sound of a door opening.

Her first thought was that Robbie had come back, that the night air had restored her to her usual calm good sense. Leaving the dog to cower in his corner, Helen started toward the hall. She heard footsteps beyond the door.

But at the door, still inside the room, she stopped again. These footsteps were not from the stairs, but from the other direction. They were coming along the hall from her mother's bedroom.

Helen stepped back and closed her door, turning the key in the lock. She was shaking with terror. It felt as if the room had turned to ice, and she clasped her arms about herself in a sudden frenzy of shivering.

How stupid she had been, not to have realized: each time it had been more, more vivid, more complete. She should have known that this time it would go beyond the others in some way.

She went back to Tiger. That poor creature was in a dreadful state. He was pressed so tightly against the wall, she wondered that he hadn't hurt himself. Helen approached, wanting to gather Tiger into her arms, not only to comfort him but to take solace from the feel of living flesh next to her own.

But the poor animal was crazed with terror. He showed his teeth in a snarl and would certainly have bitten her if Helen had tried to pick him up. He did not seem even to recognize her.

In the next moment, however, Helen had forgotten the dog. A sound from outside drove every other thought from her mind and she turned toward the locked door. The room was even colder now than it had been before.

I am calm, Helen told herself. *Maybe I am even dreaming this, as I dreamed those other things. Or did I dream them? Is this what they mean by cold chills going up and down your spine? It starts all the way down, in my bowels, and goes all the way up and back down again, in flashes, like something alive.*

She wanted to shout at whatever was outside her door, to tell it to go away. To ask, even, who or what was out there, but she had no voice with which to speak. Her voice had been frozen inside her with the cold.

Robbie, Robbie, why did you leave me?

Nothing happened. The seconds dragged by. She imagined she heard the old clock in the downstairs hall ticking, though that would have been impossible. It might have been an hour, or only minutes, that she stood there, staring at the door, waiting for something to happen. She told herself that the intelligent thing, the right thing that Robbie would do, was to walk to the door, to turn the key in the lock and open the door, and face whatever was out there.

She even told herself, *Probably there is nothing at all there, and an empty hall would relieve me of this fear, and I could quietly pack up a few things and leave this house, and check into a hotel room somewhere in town for the rest of the night. For the rest of my life, even.*

She knew, however, that even if her feet would carry her across the room, nothing under God's blue heaven would ever make her open that door.

Finally, after she knew not how long she waited, there was a sound. Not, as she might have expected, a knock or a rattle or a bang, but something far more terrible than any of those: a whimper.

Something beyond the door mewled, like a baby crying faintly. The way her mother used to cry when her father had done something hurtful.

It whimpered, and scratched at the door, scratched on the wood with long fingernails.

Helen thought, *I am going to scream. I cannot help myself, I am going to scream.*

But she did not scream. She moved away from the door, stepping backward because she could not take her eyes off it, until like the dog she was pressed against the far wall.

She waited. And waited.

And waited.

16

She must have dozed, or perhaps she had actually fainted standing up, pressed against the wall. She did not know exactly when it ended. She was gradually aware of the room growing light with dawn, and suddenly she realized that the cold had gone. It was still cool, true, but this was more a normal nightly chill. That unearthly iciness had faded at some time or other without her quite being aware of it.

She began to rub the circulation back into her arms and to walk about the room. She looked at the door and listened, but she could hear nothing from beyond it, and finally she was sure that the ordeal was really over, at least for this one night.

It took some minutes more, though, before she was able to summon the courage to cross the room and actually open the door to the hall.

There was nothing there. The house lay still about her, presumably empty. She had survived another onslaught of that terror. Without, as things had turned out, Robbie's help.

It would be the last such night. She promised herself that. She meant to leave the house today, during the daylight hours, never to return. And she did not care what anyone thought or said about that. And after all, what could anyone do? This could no longer be attributed to her imagination, nor could it be regarded as a barometer of her sanity. Robbie had been here, too, and she had been frightened out of her wits. She could not deny that she had been so frightened she had dashed away.

Helen felt a bit lightheaded from lack of sleep, and from the feeling of relief that the ordeal was momentarily over. She came back into her room and went to the window, flinging it open and breathing deeply of the crisp morning air.

She had forgotten about the dog until her eyes fell on him as she brought her head back from the window. Tiger lay in the corner where he had cowered during the night. Helen called to him but there was no response.

With an eerie sinking feeling, she went to where Tiger lay, but before she reached him she knew that the dog was dead. His body was already cold to the touch. His eyes protruded, his tongue hung out of his mouth. The froth had gathered around his jaws.

The poor animal had died of fright.

* * *

She found a towel in the bathroom and, wrapping him in that, carried him down to the kitchen.

By the time she had made herself coffee and warmed her still cold hands over the kitchen range, Mrs. Hauptman had arrived.

'How do you suppose he died?' Mrs. Hauptman wondered when Helen asked her to do something with the body. The towel in which Helen had wrapped the poor creature concealed the look of terror on his face, and Mrs. Hauptman showed no interest in uncovering him.

'He was dead when I found him this morning,' Helen said evasively.

Mrs. Hauptman stared at the little bundle for a long moment, and Helen half-feared after all she was going to want to see him for herself, but finally she shrugged and said, 'Oh, well, I suppose it was something internal. I'll call the pound about him a little later. Will Miss Roberta be down soon for breakfast?'

'Miss Roberta has . . . has gone out.'

Mrs. Hauptman gave her a surprised look. 'So early? She was always one to lay abed, as I recall.'

'Something came up. Let's not wait for her, all right?'

'What time will she be back?'

'I don't know,' she said simply. 'Perhaps she won't be. Ever.'

'Never?'

'Nor will I,' Helen said. 'I have decided I want to travel. You may consider this your notice. I won't be needing your services after today.'

★ ★ ★

As it turned out, the mystery of where Robbie had gone was solved for her. She was packing when the police came to see her.

'There are some gentlemen here to see you,' Mrs. Hauptman announced in awe. It was midmorning and there still had been no word from Robbie.

It was so unlike Mrs. Hauptman to announce visitors formally, and it was so unusual for Helen to receive any, that she knew at once, instinctively, that something extraordinary had happened.

She came into the hall to find two highway patrolmen waiting there.

'Miss Sparrow?' the older of the two addressed her.

He reminded Helen of her father; not so much the way he looked — although Helen was not unaware that he was strikingly handsome in his neat, well-fitted uniform — but the way he stood, ramrod-straight, and the way he spoke. Even the look he gave Helen was cool, commanding, stern.

'Yes,' Helen said, meekly, so very softly that she felt compelled to say it again, a little louder. 'Yes.'

'Do you happen to know a Miss

Roberta Sparrow?'

'Robbie, yes, she's my sister. What is it, has something happened?'

'There's been an accident,' the officer said, speaking in that same stern, emotionless voice. 'Your sister's car went off the road, just a couple of miles from here.'

Helen took a step toward the patrolman, reaching a hand out toward him. She wanted to touch the man, to assure herself of the reality of him, of this moment. She felt drawn to him, as if to a magnet. The broad shoulders, the thick chest. To be held in those muscled arms . . . but the officer took a step backward, avoiding the touch.

'Is she . . . ?' But Helen could not bring herself to ask the question.

The outstretched hand, the faltering question, spurred the younger man to action. He stepped toward Helen, clasped her firmly by the shoulders.

'Easy,' he said. He had a gentle voice, kind, and that oddly served to restore Helen's self-control.

'I'm all right,' Helen said, taking a deep

breath. 'Tell me what happened to Robbie.'

'Your sister is dead,' the older man said flatly.

Helen thought she had known that from the moment Mrs. Hauptman had announced them, had known perhaps from the first moment that she returned to the house, that everything was moving toward something like this. She was more stunned than surprised.

'I see,' she said, and then because the patrolman still held her shoulders, she shrugged herself away from him and said, clearly, 'I am all right, really.'

The older man said, 'I'd like to ask, ma'am, if there was anything bothering your sister? A quarrel, maybe?'

Helen said, without the slightest hesitation, 'No, there were no quarrels. Why do you ask?'

'There was a witness to the accident, a man driving just behind your sister. He said it looked as if she had ... ' He faltered for just a moment. ' ... had wrecked her car deliberately. Like she might have meant to kill herself.'

17

If Helen had not before realized the power that wealth conferred upon those who possessed it, she certainly became aware of it when she pursued her plans to travel. The travel agent she found was happy to arrange every detail for her.

Everything was made as painless as possible for her. A man from the agency, as soft-talking as the doctors at the clinic had been, came to her hotel room and discussed plans with her.

They agreed that Florida was nice this time of year, and far enough away to make a good trip without going too far. When Helen informed the man that he need not worry about the expense, the travel agent was even more courteous and helpful than before.

A week later, on Christmas Day, Helen flew to Miami. She had never been there before, and she found it enchanting after the winter gloom of the past few months in New York.

Even travel was not so terrifying as it had been for her in the past. The agent took very good care of her. Whenever she wanted to go sightseeing, there was a car and driver waiting at her beck and call.

For the rest, she stayed near the hotel, one of the grand baroque ones right on the beach, and ate most of her meals there as well. The beach was crowded with visitors from up north flocking to the warmth and sunshine.

Helen went so far as to buy a swimsuit in the hotel's shop, but after donning it one day she decided she didn't feel confident enough to expose herself on the beach, and put the suit in a dresser drawer, never to be worn.

By the time she had been there a week, she found herself getting around quite nicely without the need of the car and driver, and with no more assistance than some directions or some friendly advice from someone in the hotel. It was a new feeling of independence that she had never experienced before.

She even began to think of doing some more travel after this trip. There were countless places she had dreamed of visiting in the past, without ever feeling that she was able to do so. Now she could see them all if she wished. She could spend the rest of her life traveling if she chose to do so, and she never need face returning to that house. Let it rot, for all she cared.

She wrote to Aunt Willa to tell her that she had decided the house should have gone to her after all, and a sizable chunk of the money too, and that she planned to take the necessary legal steps when she returned to New York to see to both. That, she knew, would still any doubts Aunt Willa had about her.

It was not until the moon began to wax that her nervousness returned. She knew that she had nothing to fear this time, that the things that had happened to her only happened in that house, that for once the full moon would shine upon her without bringing that terror.

Even so, she was tense and out of sorts as the evening approached, and she knew that she would be grateful when it had come and gone.

It was pointless to plan anything for that night. She knew she would be able to think of nothing else. She stayed in the hotel and had an early dinner in the dining room. The waiter — Joseph was his name — had taken a friendly interest in her since her arrival. Here, Joseph saw immediately, was a young woman, not unattractive, alone, and obviously wealthy. Joseph had set himself to catching Helen's eye. But although she had been friendly and appeared grateful for the attention, he had been unable to make her aware of him in that way.

'You weren't hungry tonight?' Joseph said, removing the plate with the almost untouched dinner.

'I'm a little tired,' Helen said, giving him a smile just faintly edged with worry. 'I think I'll make an early night of it.'

'Full moon tonight,' Joseph said, pouring her coffee. 'Very romantic. Good-looking girl like you, you ought to be out dancing. I know a place . . . '

Helen shivered at the reminder of what

night it was, and said, 'Maybe next month.'

Disappointed, Joseph watched Helen leave the dining room not much after eight o'clock. For a moment, he'd thought . . . He shrugged. He had been disappointed that his cautious pass had gotten him nowhere. But Helen hadn't closed the door on him completely, at least. She had said *next month*. Maybe he was still in the game.

Back in her room, Helen felt a headache threatening. 'It's the worrying,' she told herself, and took an aspirin and a sleeping pill and went directly to bed.

She did not know how long she slept, but it could not have been too long because when she woke she was still groggy from the sleeping pill. For a moment she did not know what had awakened her. The room was silent except for some faint noises along the corridor. An elevator door opened and closed.

Then it came again, the laughter that had penetrated even her drug-inspired sleep and roused her from its depths. The laughter that had haunted her again and again in the past. The hysterical laughter of her mother's death night.

Her horror was unimaginable. For a few minutes or so she sat motionless in bed, as if frozen in place, and that monstrous laugh rose higher and higher, seeming to come first from this direction and then from that.

Hardly knowing what she was doing, she leapt from the bed and half-ran, half-staggered to the switch by the door, flooding the room with light.

She had thought that perhaps this time it really was a dream, and that with full waking it would fade, but the laugh went on, exactly as she had heard it before, a hysterical wail rising higher in pitch as it gained in volume. Surely, surely, she thought, it must rouse the entire hotel.

She was by the chest of drawers with its gilt-framed mirror, and in the glass she saw her own reflection. She had aged so much she would hardly have recognized herself. To her own frightened eyes she looked ten, even twenty, years older than she was. Her hair was in disarray, her eyes wide and wild.

For a moment she stood there, staring at this reflection that was hers and yet not her, an image out of time, and in her ears rang that awful laugh.

It had followed her. She was a thousand miles or more away from that house and the cursed laughter had followed her.

She did not know just when she became aware that something was moving behind her. She had her back to the bed and she did not recall hearing any sound from that direction, but instinctively she glanced into the mirror and her eyes were at once fixed by what she saw in the glass.

Her father rose up from the bed in which, only seconds before, Helen had been sleeping. He was dressed in shirt and trousers and a pair of navy-blue suspenders, just as he had been the last time Helen had seen him, the night of his death.

He slid over the end of the bed, and with two or three swift, silent steps came to stand behind Helen with a death-like scowl upon his face. He stood for a moment, almost touching her, and in that moment their eyes met in the mirror.

Helen knew that in that instant she was looking into death itself. Into hell.

Her father lifted a hand as if he meant to touch her. Whether he did or not, Helen did not know. Heaven mercifully intervened, and with a sigh like that of a lover, she sank to the floor in a faint.

Part III

Police Chief Wallace's notes

18

Helen Sparrow was haunted. That was the point of the whole story.

'Officer,' she said, before she said anything else, 'I am haunted. By ghosts.'

It was little wonder, too, after what had happened to her.

★　★　★

The truth is, this is not my story to tell. I did not enter into it until it was nearly played out. I met that unfortunate creature only once, and never saw inside that house in which she had experienced such terror and such unhappiness.

True, the role that Fate had assigned me to play was a crucial one, and if I had played it as directed, some tragedy might have been averted.

I say 'might have been'; I believe that I might have given her some comfort. Who can say? That is, after all, both the glory and the downfall of man, that he sometimes fails to adhere to the rather simple roles that his creator offers him.

But it is a story that very much wants telling, and who better than I to tell it, a professional man, to whom the story, or as much of it as we are ever likely to know, was entrusted?

I who can, perhaps too late, sympathize. How many times, since the afternoon that unhappy young woman sat in my office and related her story, have I started from sleep, ears straining for . . . for what? Something unheard, unfelt, and yet perceived, something that chills the very marrow of the bones.

How many times, unnerved by a feeling of 'someone there,' have I turned and almost seen something, someone, just beyond the corner of my vision, just — but only just — out of sight?

Man may scoff and scorn, but no man lives without some secret dread that may steal upon him in the dead of the night, in the very form that will most strike horror in his heart. It has been said, and perhaps it is true, that we draw unto ourselves that which we fear the most.

Helen Sparrow was haunted by death and by the dead. Every human is haunted, and no ghost is more terrifying than one's own.

★ ★ ★

She came to my office on a Tuesday afternoon. It was only by the sheerest chance that she found me there. Five minutes more and I would have been gone, would have spent that Tuesday afternoon as I spent every other Tuesday afternoon: playing some golf with Milton Taylor. And after that, early cocktails and dinner with my wife on the one evening of the week that we set aside inviolably for one another.

Ours was a small town, and while the title 'Chief of Police' sounds impressive, the truth was that there were only four others on the entire force. There was little crime in our small upstate New York town, not like the big city to the south of us. No murders, no drug overdoses, no armed robberies. Only an occasional drunk driver, a domestic squabble now and again, some minor theft of little consequence.

I was already clearing the last of the morning's mail off my desk when the dispatcher, Grace, came in, closing the door after herself and looking altogether guilty. For the latter, she had good reason, which she quickly revealed.

'There's someone waiting to see you,' she informed me. 'A Miss Helen Sparrow.'

'I see. And does this Miss Helen Sparrow have an appointment?' I asked. 'Or some major crime to report? Something that you cannot handle?'

They were rhetorical questions. In addition to her duties as dispatcher, Grace had been functioning as the station's receptionist for almost twenty years, in which time no one had ever had an appointment on Tuesday afternoon. Not ever. And, as I have already indicated, we had no major crimes.

I had been in the process of stacking some papers to give Grace before I left. I went on with my sorting. I had already decided — indeed, it was so automatic it could hardly be called a decision — to tell her to ask Miss Sparrow to return the next day.

Grace, however, did not answer my question directly. She said, 'I think you ought to see this individual. I don't think she would come back. She seems rather beside herself.'

'About what?' I finished with the papers. 'Has she been assaulted? Robbed?'

'She says she's haunted.'

I said, surprised into attention, 'Haunted? By God. In what way haunted?'

'Haunted. By ghosts. Like the lady of Blackwood Hall.'

I had stopped fooling with the things on my desk. Of course she was right. I couldn't pass that one up. I had dealt with hallucinations before, and illusions of various kinds, but I had never actually had to cope with ghosts, despite a fascination with that subject ranging back to my earliest childhood.

For whatever reason, that is not a problem people ordinarily bring to a police station. I had never even thought of helping anyone deal with ghosts, but the thought no sooner entered my mind than I was intrigued by it.

'Call the hospital,' I said, refusing to

acknowledge Grace's triumph of judgment by looking directly at her, 'and ask them to have a room ready. I may need to send someone to see them. And show this Miss — uh, what's her name . . . ?'

Grace was nothing if not tactless. 'I've already called the hospital,' she said, going out. 'And her name is Sparrow. Helen Sparrow.'

She was back in a moment, ushering in the visitor, and ushering herself quickly out again before I could say what I was thinking.

'This is Miss Sparrow,' she said, and was gone.

I acknowledged the 'introduction,' adding, since Grace had not thought this important enough to mention, 'I'm Officer Wallace. Police Chief Wallace.'

I suggested that Miss Sparrow have a seat in the chair facing my desk.

Miss Sparrow took the chair I had indicated, hurrying to it as if to a sanctuary, and sliding down into it in such a manner that the back and the arms practically hid her from any view but mine. And I say 'sliding' deliberately. The woman seemed to lack a certain quality of solidity. I might almost have been willing to believe that she herself was a ghost.

Lest I be accused of hindsight, I have consulted the notes that I made during that initial meeting with Helen Sparrow. The very first notation that I made on the scratch pad that I keep on the desk before me was the word *furtive*, and after that, *haunted*. I had underlined the latter.

Laying aside any consideration of ghosts and visits from beyond the grave, which I prefer to do, Helen Sparrow's description of herself still seemed remarkably apt. She did indeed seem haunted. No one could look at her and not remark at once the strain that she was under, nor fail to see in her eyes the flickering gleam of fear. I should have said that she was a woman living on the brink of terror. And in very grave danger of falling over that edge.

A comparison came into my mind at once. After the Second World War, my father, then a young army doctor, had occasion to interview certain Jews who had been prisoners of the Nazis, and at his death he had left his journals to me.

Although by the time he saw these individuals they had already been released from captivity, and presumably from their persecution, he remarked that they one and all still had about them that look of anxiety, of awful expectancy. They were waiting for something dreadful to occur, something from which, despite all assurances, they were certain there would be no escape.

The young woman who had seated herself across the desk from me had very nearly this same look of horror about her, horror beyond hope.

I had made also a note of her name, and added a question mark because it seemed to me that it sounded vaguely familiar. Later, when she had talked, I recollected some of the story concerning the death of her parents. It was not in my jurisdiction, of course, but it had made rather splashy headlines for a time.

All of these initial observations, however, had been made in the course of the few seconds that it took Miss Sparrow to come across the office and seat herself.

When we were facing one another across the desk, and I had made the notes that I have remarked upon, I spoke to her.

'Now then, Miss Sparrow, What seems to be the problem?'

She said, 'I am haunted. By ghosts.'

She sat with her hands clasped in her lap so tightly that I could see the knuckles were turned white. She lowered her eyes.

'I want to be committed,' she said.

'You mean, I suppose, to a mental institution?'

Again she nodded.

'That sort of thing is usually arranged by one's family.'

'Are you saying that you cannot assist me?'

'No, not exactly. Perhaps it will help if you tell me about this — this haunting. Let me just get some information down here. Will it embarrass you to tell me your age?'

'I'm twenty-eight years old,' she said, and added without pause, 'I'm a virgin.'

I tried not to show my surprise at her age. I would have guessed it at nearly twice that figure. Now, at a second glance, I could see that what I had at first taken to be signs of her age were only further evidence of the strain under which she had apparently been living.

As to the other remark, I was at once curious as to why she had considered that information germane. I have long held the opinion that, from a criminologist's standpoint, there is no such thing as an irrelevant remark. Every remark is relevant to what is going on inside the head of the speaker, and is thus a clue to his thought processes.

If the individual is very fortunate, and is able to accumulate enough such clues that patterns begin to take shape, he is able, in effect, to 'read the mind' of another. In my opinion, when all is said and done, that is what psychiatry is about, Freud and his early toilet training notwithstanding.

In the brief pause that followed, I got the impression (I may have been mistaken) that she expected me to question her further along those lines, but for the moment I had other ideas.

'Perhaps if you told me about this

. . . haunting . . . ' I let my voice trail off expectantly.

For a moment she said nothing. Finally, she said, 'Officer Wallace, if I tell you, you will decide that I am crazy. It would save time if you simply had me committed now and were done with it.'

'That may be so,' I said, 'But that way you would deprive me of the material I need for the book I am going to write when I retire.'

I was a little disappointed that she did not take this as a joke, but seemed to be giving it serious consideration. Be that as it may, she did decide to tell me her story and began to talk in a low, monotonous voice.

I have tried herein to reconstruct that story, more or less as it took shape for me while she talked. I did not take copious notes, trusting to my memory, but I think her story made so vivid an impression that I am not likely to have forgotten much of it. I have a tape recorder in my office, on a table behind where Miss Sparrow was sitting, but when she began so abruptly to talk, I feared that it might distract her if I were to get up to get the recorder, bring it to the desk, and hook it up. I thus chose not to use it.

But I think I have gotten the story right. She did not tell me her tale in exact chronological order, and there were some points on which she remained vague, so that the reader may see for himself the questions that I had to ponder upon as the story unfolded. Perhaps the reader's conclusions will be different from mine.

19

Not only did I not have my golf game that afternoon, but I was late arriving home.

Helen Sparrow's story was fascinating. It was hardly necessary to prompt her, and in fact I spoke almost not at all.

Once, she paused and asked if she might have a glass of water, and I asked Grace to bring her one. I must give Grace credit: she had stayed as well, sacrificing what should have been her own afternoon off. She had only a husband to go home to, however, and not a golf game, which I think anyone would agree is not at all the same thing.

'If you are tired,' I said to Miss Sparrow while we waited for her glass of water, 'please tell me so and we will continue this another time.'

She gave her head a rather violent shake. 'I am tired,' she said frankly, 'but waiting until another time will not help that. No, I would rather go on.'

She seemed then suddenly to remember herself and turning about in the chair, she said, 'Oh, perhaps you have other complainants?'

'Tuesday is my free afternoon,' I told her. Grace brought the water in a paper cup. I took it from her and, after bringing it to Miss Sparrow, seated myself once again behind the desk.

She sipped in silence for a moment after Grace had gone out again. Then she said, 'I have money, you know. I can pay for your time.'

'I am a servant of the municipality. No payment is required. Nor would it be legal for me to accept it.'

She smiled, I fancied with a bit less tension than before. I think I had put her somewhat at ease. After another pause, she continued with her story. In the telling, I think she was able to relieve herself of some measure of the awful anxiety she carried about with her. I won't say she looked more relaxed, but certainly she seemed less tied in knots as the time went along.

When she spoke of the incident in the

hotel in Miami, however, she grew visibly agitated. She sat forward in her chair and at one point reached out to clasp the edge of my desk, as if she were afraid of falling. Her eyes grew so wild-looking, her whole demeanor so frantic, that I actually felt alarmed and considered interrupting her.

This mood of agitation reached a sort of climax, as it were, when she talked of the vision seen in the mirror.

'I fainted,' she said, and with that, her shoulders slumped and she fell back once again in her chair, almost as if she were imitating the faint for me. I thought that the crisis was past, although of course she remained tense and distraught.

She was silent for so long that I wondered if our interview had come to an end. Nonetheless I prompted her by saying, 'And when you regained consciousness, there was nothing in the room with you?'

She fixed her eyes on me again. There was something harsh in the look she gave me. I think she half-feared that I was ridiculing her, but my face, apparently, was bland enough to pass inspection.

'Nothing,' she said, dropping her eyes.

'This was last winter,' I said.

'Yes. I haven't been back until now. After that happened, I traveled. I traveled extensively. I couldn't bear to stay in that hotel, and I left the next morning. To be honest, I could hardly stand to stay in any one place more than a day or two. I began to receive curious letters and telegrams from my relatives — from my aunt especially. They must have really begun to wonder about my travels. I moved around so much and so fast that some of the letters were weeks late in reaching me.

'I went to New Orleans and Galveston and Phoenix, Arizona. To Los Angeles and San Francisco and Denver and Chicago. And finally I went abroad. I went to London and Copenhagen and to Athens.'

Again she paused for a long time, so that I said, anticipating what she was going to tell me, 'And did these experiences follow you?'

She sighed, so profoundly that it was as if all hope of peace was passing from her through her lips.

'A month after that incident in Miami, on the night of the next full moon, I was in Phoenix. It was quite a distance from home, further than I had ever traveled before, and I ought to have felt safe there. But as the time drew near, I began to feel really scared. I told myself not to be a damned fool, but I couldn't help myself. I was afraid those things had followed me, and I knew if I heard those screams in Phoenix, I would go on hearing them all my life. I don't think I am completely without courage, Officer, but there are limits to what flesh and blood can endure. I thought I would go stark raving mad if I heard those cries again. As the time came closer, I found myself counting the days. I could hardly sleep, I had no appetite. I sat in my room, hour after hour. The suspense was awful.

'And one night, about two or three nights before it was due, I was awake, just staring at the ceiling of my hotel room. And I knew, suddenly and irrevocably, that it would come. I was certain of it.

'And it did come. I was more than two thousand miles from that house, and I heard my mother's screams as she was murdered.

'I heard them again in Chicago, and in Athens. And if you can't help me, I am going to hear them as long as I live.'

She stopped. Her long narrative was obviously finished this time. Moreover, with its completion, she looked suddenly exhausted, even drained. I found myself wondering how long it had been since she had had something as simple sounding as a good night's sleep.

My immediate impression was that if she could just be reassured sufficiently to allow her a day or two of real rest, we would be well on our way to solving her problems.

Afterward, I was to berate myself bitterly for taking so simplistic a view. I can defend my actions to myself only by recalling again that there was nothing about Helen Sparrow to indicate that she was in any physical danger.

Yes, she had seen and heard some incredible things, if her story was to be believed, and oddly I found that I did believe it, but nothing physical had happened. Even with that climactic vision of her father, she had fainted before the instant in which her father might actually have touched her. And as for that hand which had supposedly shaken her awake at night, well, she had been sleeping when that happened. That might only have been the hangover from a dream, as she herself half suspected.

Moreover, for all her fear and anxiety and strain, Miss Sparrow did not give the impression of being out of control, or even approaching that state. In fact, considering all that she had been through, I thought her remarkably well restrained. I think that I myself in her shoes might have been a blubbering idiot by this time.

I did not, therefore, even had it been within my purview, believe in the necessity of actually having Miss Sparrow committed to a mental institution. I did feel that she badly needed rest and I thought she could get the needed rest in a medical hospital, in clinical surroundings. She had been confined before, in that clinic, and had found herself largely free from anxiety or from strange happenings.

I believe this often happens. For some persons, who are insecure or beset by anxiety, a clinical atmosphere alone works as a tonic, giving them a sense of reassurance.

It was already late in the day. Whatever arrangements were to be made had to be made at once. It would have been cruel to ask Miss Sparrow to come back another day when she so desperately sought relief now, and I felt confident that I could give it.

I asked Grace, who still lingered in the outer office, to phone the local hospital, and arrange a check-in for Miss Sparrow, and a room in the psychiatric wing.

'I am going to take you to a hospital,' I told Miss Sparrow when I came back into my office. In answer to the question in her eyes, I added, 'You will be in the psychiatric ward. It is very much the same as being in a mental hospital, except that it is a bit less confining.'

She offered no objections to my arrangements. In fact, when I was ready to leave and she rose to join me, she confirmed my earlier opinion of her physical condition: she looked utterly spent.

'How long has it been since you've really slept?' I asked, and then, thinking that might be a dangerous subject to pursue at the moment, I said, 'Never mind. They'll take good care of you where you're going, have no fear of that. And the food is excellent, all those old jokes to the contrary. You'll be very comfortable, I assure you.'

I had no reservations about arranging for her the most deluxe accommodation the hospital could offer. She was, after all, a woman of considerable wealth, and in any event I thought the hapless creature was entitled to some comfort at this stage of things.

In the entire time from the completion of her story until I left her at the hospital, Miss Sparrow spoke very little. No more, in fact, than was quite necessary. There was a lifeless quality about her, almost an air of resignation, which I attributed to extreme fatigue. I had an idea she had summoned up nearly the last of her resources to bring herself to me and tell her story, and that momentarily at least she was completely exhausted.

The administrator of the hospital is an old friend of mine and so I was able to make short work of having Helen Sparrow installed in a private room, very much off to herself. My questions earlier in my office had elicited the information that her luggage was in a room at a local hotel, and I had directed Grace to go there, settle up the bill, and to bring Miss Sparrow's belongings to her.

So when at last I started for home, I thought that everything had been taken care of. If I felt any uneasiness, it was because of that last question Miss Sparrow had asked me.

'Can't you stay here?' she asked when I was preparing to leave her. 'Just for this one night?'

I smiled reassuringly and patted her hand as if she were a child, and promised that I would see her the very next day. I fully intended to do so. I was already savoring how I would confound my colleagues with this one.

As I was leaving, the head nurse accosted

me to ask if there were any special instructions regarding the patient. I suggested a
mild dose of Nembutal, assuming the doctor
was agreeable, although frankly I thought
that in her state of exhaustion, surrounded
by the tranquility of the clinic, she would
probably sleep soundly without any help.

'All she needs in the way of medical
attention, in my opinion,' I said, 'is rest.
Try to see that she is not disturbed.'

This was a psychiatric ward, of course,
where some patients tended to be violent,
so it was necessary for the nurse to ask if
any restriction was called for.

'She will need no restrictions,' I assured
her. 'This patient is not violent. Just see
that she gets rest.'

I went home.

20

All of these activities had carried me through the afternoon and well into the evening. It was later than usual when I arrived home. Eleanor, my wife, had been crocheting. She got up from the sofa as I came in, looking a little anxious.

'I was beginning to think something had happened to you,' she said, returning my kiss.

'Something did. A most interesting visitor,' I said. 'Is there time for a cocktail before dinner?'

'Of course. I have them ready.' She went to the bar and proceeded to pour a pair of crystal-clear martinis into stemmed glasses.

While she poured and I removed my tie preparatory to settling into my favorite chair, she said, 'I had a strange day myself.'

'Nothing too unpleasant, I hope.'

'No, just a lot of little things. Saks delivered the wrong coat. Can you imagine, at their prices? And I've lost my address book. How on earth can you lose an address book, especially one that big? And Marge Fisher was here all afternoon, I couldn't get her out the door.'

'That in itself would unnerve me,' I said, sitting down gratefully. She brought the glasses across the room, handing me one. I took a sip. It was her usual perfect martini.

'Umm, delicious,' I said.

'Thank you. Marge would say it's the full moon. About everything going wrong, I mean.' She took her own chair and picked up the crocheting she had laid aside when I came in.

I felt an eerie tingling at the back of my neck. I had often heard of that sensation, but I had never experienced it before. I suppose that all men, however highly educated, retain some superstitious inklings.

I looked at her across our living room and said, 'But it isn't the full moon.'

'Why, of course it is.' She was surprised by my statement.

'I glanced at my calendar when I was leaving the station. I thought the full moon was a whole week off.'

'That calendar on the wall just inside the door? I'll bet you haven't turned a leaf on that calendar in five months. Of course it's the full moon. It's up by now. Go see for yourself.'

I did just that. I went to the doors that opened onto the tiny balcony of our apartment, and stepped outside.

Eleanor was quite right. The moon was a round silver disk. It was a trick of the imagination, of course, but I could almost fancy as I looked up at it that those features of its surfaces that appear to give it a face were arranged in an ironic smile.

'Robert? What is it?' Eleanor had followed me across the room, although there was hardly room for both of us on the miniature balcony. 'Is something wrong?'

'I'm afraid so.' I put my martini down on the nearest table and went directly to the phone. It seemed to take forever for my call to get through to the floor nurse in the psychiatric ward. She was a new girl, new to me at least, and it took a few seconds more to establish my identity.

'I brought a woman in this evening,' I told her, 'a Miss Helen Sparrow. I'm afraid she is going to require more attendance than I thought. Tell the physician that she needs to be heavily sedated, to begin with. And she must not be left alone.'

'I checked Miss Sparrow's room quite some time ago,' the voice on the phone informed me, 'and she was already deeply asleep. She seemed to be suffering from exhaustion.'

'I don't care if she is asleep. Wake her. Give her triple the dose of Nembutal.'

'Well, that of course will be up to the doctor.'

'Tell him I said this is urgent. And I want someone with her at all times for the remainder of the night. Is that clear? She is not to be left alone for a moment.'

I could tell from the tone in which the nurse agreed that she thought probably it was I who was a bit mad, but I hardly cared what she thought. My thoughts were solely for that young woman who had entrusted herself to my care.

'I'll have the attending physician call

you back,' she said rather primly.

'Please do,' I said.

I hung up the phone. Eleanor brought me my martini again and I took a healthy swallow from it.

'Robert?' she said.

'Umm, yes.' I was lost for a moment in my own thoughts. I could not escape the feeling that things had gone wrong, past my power to correct them.

I was not surprised then when the phone rang only a minute or two later. I think I remained by the phone precisely because I had been expecting bad news.

It was the floor nurse from the hospital. She was calling to tell me that Miss Sparrow was gone.

'I have no idea where she went,' she said. Her voice, probably because she was frightened, had a whining quality that made me wince. 'We're checking the floor now but it looks as if she's left the hospital.'

'I shouldn't doubt it,' I said sharply. I was mentally cursing myself for every kind of fool.

The nurse waited for some further instructions from me. When it became apparent that they were not forthcoming, she asked, 'Should I call someone? The police?'

'What? What's that? The police?' The suggestion brought me from the stunned state into which I had fallen. 'I *am* the police, you bloody fool.' I slammed the receiver down.

But who could we call? I asked myself silently. And tell them what? That a young woman had gotten loose, a young woman who was haunted?

'She's gone,' I said to Eleanor.

'Who?'

I thought for a moment. Suddenly I snapped my fingers and said, 'I think I know where.'

'Robert, I really don't . . . '

I finished my martini in a gulp and started toward the door. I paused to look back. Eleanor was staring after me, completely bewildered.

'Come on,' I said, grabbing our coats from the closet. 'I'll explain everything while we drive.'

'Do you think I should come?' she asked, already crossing the room.

'We've always spent Tuesday evenings together,' I said, and gave her a coat.

★ ★ ★

It is foolish to hold oneself completely responsible for things that happen to go wrong. I suspect needless guilt is responsible for more of the mental ills that befall individuals than any other problem.

Still, I could not help berating myself as we went. If only I'd had a bit of foresight, I would not have left Miss Sparrow under such casual care.

Fortunately, in the course of our interview I had questioned her about the whereabouts of her family home, the house in which these events had taken place. I had not only the address of the house but a fair idea of its location. It would take at least an hour, perhaps closer to two, to reach it. I was only assuming, of course, that this was where she had headed. What we might find when we got there I could not even venture to guess.

As I drove, as fast as I was able, I told Eleanor the story that I had heard that afternoon for the first time. I had to abbreviate it, and there were certain details that I thought it discreet to omit, but even without these it made an odd tale to tell, racing through the night on the expressway. Above, watching our journey with that mocking smile, was the moon. Again and again I found myself glancing upward through the windshield at that silver countenance.

'That poor child,' Eleanor said when I had finished my narrative.

'Yes, yes, it's a dreadful story,' I replied. I was looking for street signs. We were nearly there by this time. It had taken most of two hours.

'Robert, tell me something. Do you believe . . . ?' Eleanor paused. She sounded embarrassed by her question. 'Do you think the ghosts were real?'

'Real?' I found my street and turned down it. 'What is more real than fear, than thought, pray tell me? What in the flesh could be more terrifying than the fears of the mind? She was really terrified, I can tell you that. Blast it, where is that street?'

We had come to an intersection. It should have been the one I was looking for, with the street leading up to Helen Sparrow's house, but according to the street signs it was not.

I stopped at the corner in an agony of indecision. We were close, I knew that. And always haunting me was the fear that I had made a mistake; that she wouldn't be here at all. It was only a hunch that had brought me to the house in which she had suffered so.

'Robert, look.' Eleanor spoke very softly, which with her always means she is alarmed, and she put one hand on my arm.

I followed her glance. At first I saw nothing. But suddenly I realized the significance of the glow illuminating the sky in the direction in which Eleanor pointed, a flickering, sometimes red, sometimes yellow glow.

Just how I knew it was that house that was burning, I cannot say. It may have been pure intuition, or perhaps while I drove through the night I had been expecting just such a conclusion as this.

I only know that I did not hesitate but turned up the street in the direction of the glow. Following it, I came soon to the wall and the gate that she had described to me. The gates were closed. When I got out to open them I heard in the distance the keen wail of sirens. Someone had already called the fire department.

They would be too late, however. I could see that as we drove at breakneck speed up the drive to the house and skidded to a halt, jumping out of the car. Already the heat was intense, as the flames leaped skyward from the gabled roof.

I ran to the big front door, braving the heat, only to find the door locked. As I should have known it would be had I stopped to think. I rang the bell, which was scorching hot to the touch, and pounded upon the door, shouting Helen's name, all in vain.

Finally, in desperation, I ran around the house to the side. Eleanor tried to run along with me but she was having a difficult time of it with her heels in the thick grass. Finally, with an oath I didn't think I'd ever heard her say before, she paused long enough to kick her shoes off.

Throughout this scene there was an eerie feeling of *déjà vu*. I had none of that sense of trying to find my way around a strange property. Rather, it was as if I knew exactly where I was going. As if I were being guided.

I found the stack of firewood, just where I knew from her description that it would be, and with a piece of wood I broke out the panes of glass in the French doors leading into the den.

But as the glass went, perhaps giving more air to the fire within, a wall of flame rose up before me, blocking any possible entry to the house by that route. I could feel and smell the hair burning on my arms as I put them up for protection. I'd heard people describe the roar of a fire as if it were the cry of an angry beast, but I had never heard it before. It was deafening.

'Robert, for God's sake, come away!' Eleanor screamed, tugging at my arm. 'It's too late.'

She was right, although my mind had stubbornly resisted this truth. I let her lead me from the house until we were some distance away on the lawn. I took off my coat, which had been scorched, and wiped the sweat from my face with it.

I started to say something, but Eleanor suddenly cocked her head, her eyes enormous in the whiteness of her face, and said, 'Listen.'

I tried to listen, but at that moment the fire trucks came up the drive and their sirens drowned out anything else.

'What was it?' I asked.

She gave me a peculiar look. 'I thought I heard someone laughing,' she said.

'For God's sake, where?'

She glanced toward the burning house. 'In there.'

For a moment a cold chill went up and down my spine, despite the heat from the holocaust.

But almost at once my better judgment came to my rescue and I dismissed the suggestion as impossible

'You must have imagined it,' I said. The house was by this time an inferno in which no living creature could possibly still survive.

No living creature.

* ⋆ ⋆

Was Helen Sparrow dead? I do not know. Nobody was found in the ashes of the house, but that destruction was so complete that I do not know if I can cite that as evidence.

So far as I can say, no one has ever heard from her since. I contacted Doctor Martin, who had not seen or heard from her since he sent Helen home from the Ville de Valle.

I discreetly contacted her relatives also, but with no success.

No one had anything to tell me.

Even assuming, however, that she was in the house when it burned, I still could not say what the outcome of that might have been for her. Whether she ceased to live or had begun to live with that event, or whether she was still haunted or not, I could not even hope ever to know for sure.

In any event, there is no real evidence she was in the house when it burned. For all I know, she may be living now in some sleepy Mexican village, the true expatriate

in sandals and faded blue jeans. Perhaps she has bleached her hair, as she once contemplated doing, and changed her wardrobe, and with the confidence acquired from liquor or drugs, now mingles in some glittering beach city with the beautiful people.

And perhaps they wonder, 'Who is this mysterious young woman in our midst?' They may well call her eccentric.

They neither mind too much, however, nor question too loudly, because she is generous with her food and her liquor and her company, for she is rarely alone.

Only, once a month she will withdraw. When the moon grows fat and rich in the sky, they will not see her in their lavish haunts. She will be alone then, in the soul's black night, suffering a pain that no amount of drug or liquor can mitigate.

Perhaps — but these are only fantasies that I spin, maybe to ease my own sense of guilt.

There was nothing more that I could do when my investigations, such as they were, found no trace of her. In one sense or another, she was gone. The house was

gone. Nothing remained but the ghosts.

And they do remain. One is born afraid, and dies afraid. So long as one lives, one's ghosts will haunt him. Or her.

They are oneself.